STORIES
OF an
IMAGINARY
childhood

Library of American Fiction

Melvin Jules Bukiet
Stories of an Imaginary Childhood

Rebecca Goldstein
Mazel

Curt Leviant
Ladies and Gentlemen, the Original Music of the Hebrew
Alphabet *and* Weekend in Mustara: *Two Novellas*

Stories of an Imaginary Childhood

Melvin Jules Bukiet

THE UNIVERSITY OF WISCONSIN PRESS

The University of Wisconsin Press
1930 Monroe Street
Madison, Wisconsin 53711

www.wisc.edu/wisconsinpress/

3 Henrietta Street
London WC2E 8LU, England

Library of Congress Cataloging-in-Publication Data

Bukiet, Melvin Jules.

Stories of an imaginary childhood / Melvin Jules Bukiet.

pp.   cm. — (Library of American fiction)

Contents: The virtuoso—Levitation—The apprentice—The quilt and the bicycle—
Sincerely, yours—The woman with a god—Ventriloquism—The blue-eyed Jew—
New words for old—Virginity—Nurseries—Torquemada.

ISBN 0-299-18074-3

1. Jews—Poland—Fiction. 2. Holocaust, Jewish (1939–1945)—Fiction. 3.
Poland—Social life and customs—Fiction.

I. Title. II. Series.

PS3552.U398 S76   2002

813'.54—dc21   2002022781

Some of the stories collected in this volume were previously published in slightly
different form in the following journals: "The Virtuoso" in *Columbia;* "Levitation"
and "Sincerely, Yours" in *The Kenyon Review;* "The Quilt and the Bicycle" in *Confrontation;* "Ventriloquism" in *Southwest Review;* "The Blue-Eyed Jew" in *Seattle Review;* "New Words for Old" in *Story Quarterly;* "Virginity" in *Antaeus;* "Nurseries"
in *Bomb.*

To my father and our family

Contents

Stories of an Imaginary Childhood

The Virtuoso

*S*how me a Jewish home without a prodigy and I'll show you an orphanage. So thought the great sage and musician of Proszowice, me, as I made sounds like the slaughter of swine on my new violin. My chest felt as hollow as the body of the instrument, my head as awkwardly cocked as the scroll, my nerves wound as tight as the strings. Yet worse was the offense to my aesthetic sensibility, worst of all the fact that I was producing it.

On the last Saturday in July we were strolling home from synagogue, skirting the banks of the river, approaching my favorite tree. Wild and shaggy, the willow's trunk was bare beneath a gaping knothole. As always, I peered into the cavernous recess, where I imagined forest sprites hidden the way one's other self hides in a mirror. As always, I knocked, listening carefully for the faint, woodsy echo.

My younger brother tugged at my sidelocks, but I was too mature to chase him. I walked ahead to where my parents were chatting with neighbors. Mrs. Horowitz, jealous perhaps of the competition her three unmarried daughters had to face, was bad-mouthing Rebecca. "That hussy, she has the nerve to come to shul dressed like some Venetian. It's outrageous." To which Isaac the Millionaire replied, "And the cantor's voice. It gets worse every week. I don't know why we don't hire a substitute. Any croaker will do." My parents nodded as one. I scooted ahead and was first to arrive home. I opened the closet door to put away my good blue jacket, but the cat had been napping there during our absence. Awakened, she jumped and disturbed the ancient violin case, which tottered and fell.

Frayed at the edges, exhibiting straw thatch beneath its nubby black surface, the iron-maiden-shaped box had sat in our hall closet for years. The instrument had been my father's and his father's before him. Legend had it that it originally came from fifteenth-century Spain, where it had played to the accompaniment of the Exile. It had led the column of Jews to the border, out, and across

Europe, adopting the rhythms of the countries through which it passed, the minuet, waltz, and mazurka, until it arrived here in the land of the final diaspora, the home of the Yiddish lullaby.

Sometimes word of the outside world penetrated our closet, and the sleeping beast would stir, as if its strings were vibrating within their dark, velvet confinement. This would happen whenever another young Heifetz blossomed from the Pale. The news, delayed two years in transit, would cause a ripple of hungry expectation among the local parents, and some unlucky youth would be chosen as the sacrificial victim on the musical altar. Because of the illustrious history of the instrument in our house, I had always been a candidate for this dubious honor. "Please, what I can do with your son," implored Mrs. Hemtobble, teacher, keeper of the archives, and high priestess of the monstrous harmonic rites.

The only thing that kept me from such a fate was my parents' fear of the secular. Were I to evince a truly superior talent (and was there any doubt?) I would have to continue my post-Hemtobble studies in Cracow, that notorious cauldron of sin. It was well known that I was susceptible to influence and to the vagaries of the imagination.

You might think that for just this reason I would have dived into the mysteries of point and counterpoint, but fantasy as I would, I knew that I would never outlearn our matriarchal maestro. I was not one to hum a tune or tap my feet, nor could I tell a sharp from a flat to save my life. Not only would I never be a master, I could never be a good student. Lamentably, my family's faith in their son was too great to be swayed by mere facts, and I grudgingly awaited the consequences of my birth.

All this raced through my mind as the violin case was plummeting through the dense closet air toward my face. It was no musical instinct, I swear, that brought my arms up for the catch. It was strictly self-preservation, but had I known the result of this gesture I would willingly have accepted a bump on the head. Instead, my hands automatically gripped the plunging instrument, one cradling it underneath, the other on top, in a grim parody of the correct playing posture.

My mother entered the front door and gasped.

I felt as if I had been caught in some perverse act of my imagination. I stammered and blushed, and finally shoved the stupid thing back on the shelf where it belonged, but the look of smitten surprise never left my mother's face.

That night murmurs of intense discussion emanated from the kitchen. I listened through the pipe that carried winter heat from the stove.

"Did you see the way he held it?"

"But he's only a child."

"But did you see the way he held it?"

"Barely twelve, how could we send him away?"

"Next year he will be a Bar Mitzvah. He could study here until then, and then. . . ."

"I know, a man, legally a man," my father conceded. "It would be a sin for us to restrain him, but still . . ."

"A veritable Heifetz," my mother whispered.

And so the odious thing was officially removed from its place of storage. I felt as if I were present at a disinterment. The dusty, moldy box was set on the kitchen table. I snapped open the rusty latch, let escape the noxious vapors. The hinges creaked, and the velvet skin unfolded to reveal the secret anatomy.

The ribs of the body showed through the taut, lacquered tissue, which glistened and seemed to draw all of the light in the room to it. The chest was perforated by twin vents, through which it breathed. The vertebraed neck culminated in the skull, from which the strings descended like strands of silver hair.

"Your grandfather should have been here," my grandmother said.

My mother looked at it as fondly as she would a newborn infant. "Try, my darling," she said, and I wasn't sure if she was addressing me or the corpse. As if on cue, the rest of the family, including the cat, inched back, leaving me alone at the table.

I should have known better, but I was weak and could not resist. Made confident by my home, I felt invincible. I grasped the violin firmly, my left hand curling around its spine to sneak up on the jugular. I lifted it to my chin, smelling the chins of generations of unfulfilled prodigies. I took the bow. I rapped the table. I slit its throat.

The cat howled and bolted from the room.

My mother said, "A few lessons will work wonders."

Mrs. Hemtobble was coming; I was doomed. "Vun. Two. Sree. Feir," she would count, and ferociously recount, "Vun. Two . . ." while bow tangled, strings burst, and melody flew like a fireplace cinder to the winds. A number of my friends had been singed in this method. They were recognizable a mile off, haggard, distracted, muttering to themselves. They were, in fact, a lot like Mr. Hemtobble, our shoemaker, who sat at his bench all day, tapping at his leather in his wife's inflexible cadence.

Though she had married the frail cobbler whose name she bore, Mrs. Hemtobble's constitution was the same as her brother's, our butcher, Cohen. Between the one, with his blood-stained cleaver, and the other, they haunted our dreams. She was a big woman, with features like the chipped bark of the hollow tree and a club foot that beat relentlessly in my brain for a week before my first lesson. It therefore came as little surprise when my auditory premonition slid over the boundary from nightmare to daylight. I ran to open the door for the heavy, stumping terror, hoping that this conciliatory gesture would somehow lighten my sentence. My appeal was denied. She looked down on me like the army officer who came to steal children for the Polish militia. "So you are the new student."

"Yes, Ma'am," I answered humbly, wishing to fly.

"So, then where iss it?"

I pointed helplessly at the closet.

"Well then, so get. I am to teach you for an hour, and you have already wasted thirty seconds. . . . Hurry!"

Exactly two minutes later she said, "To hold the instrument properly. It is not a club," and reversed the natural bent that had so fatally impressed my dear mother. Shoulders, elbows, wrists, and other less movable joints were poked and prodded to conform to the violin's technique. My fingers were stretched farther than ever the Lord intended. And of course the bow was set at the most uncomfortable possible angle. How or why Amati invented such a grotesque device, I will never know.

Then came the instructions, a pageful of lines, dots, and strange designs that might just as well have been Babylonian. Notwithstanding the qualms of reason, Mrs. Hemtobble was determined to enlighten me. "This," she said, "iss the E." She pointed to and simultaneously plucked one of the strings. It had the sound of crystal. "This," she said, "iss the A." It had the sound of ivory. "This," she said, "iss the D." It had the sound of mahogany. "And this," she said, "iss the G." It had the sound of gold. I felt like a commoner being introduced to royalty.

I learned the stroke, down, across, and then back away from their majesties in a smooth, steady wail. Most importantly, I learned the Hemtobble trademark, the dreaded "Vun. Two." The martinet drilled me in her system until I became a walking metronome. Under her tutelage my very pulse deferred to the law of the beat. "On the E now. Vun. Two. Sree. Feir. Quickly try the A. Two. Sree. Feir. Elbow up. Sree. Feir. Vun . . ."—and on and on, over and over, so that after my first hour's lesson I felt as if I had been washed in a tub of scalding hot water, rinsed, wrung, and hung out to dry.

Six afternoons a week, I would trudge down the corridor past my father's store and my mother's kitchen to the "music room." This was a small, glassed-in porch or pantry full of the familiar odors of onions, potatoes, and home-canned vegetables, but to me it seemed a hideous torture chamber under some medieval castle.

The music stand, like a rack, held an open sheet of the notes that I would make scream.

Usually the mere sight of my long-toed crawl to the rear of the house was enough to bring the cat running at breakneck speed. She would circle the porch, as if testing its acoustical properties, and then settle and gaze up at me with idiotic admiration. Likewise my human following would hearken if I so much as crooked a pinkie in their direction. This, I think, was the most discouraging aspect of my career. I was not modest. I was keenly aware of my better qualities, and had the sounds I created been beautiful I would have been the first to acknowledge them from a well-deserved pedestal. The unfortunate truth was that, despite many hours of diligent practice, my execution no more resembled melody than pigs. But I was the dutiful son of loving parents, and so I continued to let the bow whine its length along the four strings and back again, and my family continued to ooh and to ahh, and the cat continued to attend me with tone-deaf devotion, and I hated every second of it.

I tried to explain this to my parents, but even as the words left my mouth I could see their failure to comprehend. My father may have had intimations of the truth, but he was under the influence of my mother's dreams. In her eyes our kitchen was transformed into the theater, and I was her personal Heifetz.

It was Heifetz to the left of me, Heifetz to the right. Did I know that he had been only three when he began to play? That he was seven when he performed for the crown princes of Europe? That by my age he had bought his parents a summer house in the Crimea? Did I know? Heifetz!

And my grandmother mimed a sleepy fiddler.

I stood there glaring at my loving audience, humiliated by their unwavering loyalty. I could have smashed the violin on the hard edge of the kitchen table, but they still would not have believed me.

"What do you mean you don't want to play? Didn't we see for ourselves the way you held it?"

"Can't you hear for yourselves the way that I play it?"

"You have a talent. You reached for the case."

"It fell down from the closet shelf. The cat knocked it off."

"So now he blames the cat. Who next, the Baal Shem Tov? Nonsense! The lessons will continue."

Every Monday and Thursday the Corporal would march up to our front door, nod curtly to my father, and lead me to the back room. Her lopsided step became as familiar as the cat's hushed paw, but whereas the latter irritated me all out of proportion to the sound it produced, the loud thumping deformity was oddly reassuring. I began to look forward to Mrs. Hemtobble's lessons.

"For this I came? You did not practice two minutes, let alone two hours. . . . Since when does a third finger look like a dog sleeping on a railroad track? You know what happens. Splat!"

Yes, indeed, splat, rasp, squawk, and the wolf tone, where the note inexplicably jumped an octave—like my voice. What I created was not music; it was noise, and I gave thanks that someone could see this. I appreciated Mrs. Hemtobble's justified scorn as much as my parents did my illegitimate art.

"Now we must begin from the beginning. Vun. Two. Sree. Feir."

Always respectful, I strove to please. Make no mistake, I was still bad, but maybe less awful. The pigs in the box now snuffled, occasionally varying the pattern and pitch of their squeals. Sometimes they were almost happy, rooting about the lower octaves, grunting and rolling in the muddy sound until their farmer grabbed one to boil for lard, at which signal the usual round of squeals recommenced. In this fashion I progressed from scales to ditties to ballads to a nearly discernable rendition of the national anthem.

A growing boy, I was already too large for the adorable shoes of the innumerable Jaschas, Mischas, and other diminutive Jews packing them in at the concert halls of the capital. Still, I persevered, training my fingers to scamper up and down the musical ladder like a demented spider while my arms made graceless figure eights in midair. I learned *Rosetta from Odessa*, *The Little Goat Boy*, and a simplified version of *Wanderlust*. But if the brutalization of my

9

ears had ceased, my heart was no less troubled. Between the tolerable and the competent was a gap, between the competent and the sublime a chasm. Aware of this, my parents nonetheless expected the music of the spheres. Incredibly, that's what they heard.

Only my teacher told me the truth. Her wattles of flesh quivered with indignation, her lips with derision. "So who tells you to exhale on high C? If it took you as long to breathe as it does to think you'd be dead already. Now, we will persist until you get it right. Otherwise, I promise we'll never move on to *The Spin Ink Song*."

Twice every session, Mrs. Hemtobble referred to *The Spin Ink Song*. She held it over me like a carrot before a horse. It was the prize all her pupils received once they mastered their basic skills, after the scales, after the simpleminded melodies, one step prior to music. At the rate I was climbing, I would never see that elevated plateau, but I was resigned to my clumsy, earthbound status.

Actually I was beginning to feel a measure of contentment scraping away to the harangues of my teacher, when she too betrayed me. It was during the inauspicious debut of *My Red Rubber Ball* that she let slip the mask of contempt, beneath which lay expectations of that worst of all heroes, Heifetz. Like the subject of my latest piece, my bow jumped haphazardly across four strings, my fingers splayed out in a desparate, ineffective reach. Even the cat's dumb homage was easy, but my stern coach's thickly powdered head swayed happily to the spastic rhythm. Her response: "Very lively. It could have been neater, but all in all . . . well . . . anyway. Here is your next assignment." The sheaf of pages had a title, a half-known banner that took a moment to sink in, *The Spinning Song*. So this was the much touted, mispronounced opus. It was a slap in the face.

"I don't think I'm ready."

"You must practice extra hard for the next week."

She might have said a day, or a minute for that matter. It would take me at least two weeks to slog through the most rudimentary number, let along this imposing musical edifice. Longer and more complex than anything I had yet tackled, it made use of three bow and four finger movements, and—horrors!—a Vun-and-a-half change of tempo. But Mrs. Hemtobble was adamant, and, most disconcertingly, for a reason: she thought I could do it!

I clenched my teeth and set to work, but not without dreams of the vengeance I would wreak on the devil that led me astray. I would use its own strings to tie it to the bow, which I would plant as a stake, at which I would burn the seductive instrument. I would use its smirking, curlicued ∫ holes to fill it with water to drown it. I would crush its proud shell with a stone—anything, I thought, as I continued to practice, for I was a dutiful boy.

Alone, amid the rotting, fermenting vegetables of the back porch, my right hand guided the silken horsehairs over the taut metal quartet, which my left hand dextrously fingered. I repeated the intricate pattern so many times that I no longer needed to look, hardly needed to listen. Like Daniel in the lions' den, I made my peace with the beast from the hall closet. But at what price? The more I knew, the more I knew I lacked. The sweeter the sound, the deeper the wound; the closer to Heifetz, the larger he loomed. I lost track of time, and my sunny atelier could have been a coal mine or the inside of a hollow tree. I was exhausted. I wished to surrender, but one look at my teacher told me there was no chance. She was rapt in anesthetic bliss—she and the cat. We were all victims, lulled by the poisonous refrain of the ancient violin. "Please," I begged.

"Vun more time," she said. "But," her expression brightened inanely, "for you, a surprise . . ." and she opened the door, behind which my family stood in an awkward, eager bunch. They smiled nervously and filed in with a shy respect I neither deserved nor desired. This was to be my first official recital. "Hey," I wanted to shake them. "This is me, your son, your brother. My name is not Jascha!"

The same old battle between obligation and independence waged, with, I confess, the same result. Lacking the strength to chastise myself, I lashed the piglets mercilessly. My arm was a blur of such useless vigor that a string sprung back into a curly tail, and the remaining little swine oinked their hearts out—andante, allegro, staccato—until the massacre finally came to its foregone crescendo.

The applause was deafening.

It was past my bedtime. My cheek nuzzled the soft wood contours of the body beside me, my hand sought its magic. I could not stay memories of my pilgrimage from innocence to initiation to the reaping of unjust rewards. Worse yet, I could auger but more of the same. From my immediate family, my audience would widen to include cousins, neighbors, and strangers, at which stage my own runtish doubts were bound to be confirmed. I was as proud of our racial predilection for beauty as Heifetz's mother, but the gift was not mine. Love had stopped my loved ones' ears; only silence could open them.

Best for all concerned. I slipped on my clothes and tiptoed downstairs. To the right was the music room; to the left the kitchen, the store—and the river. For a moment I hesitated, but the cat sped through my legs in its dash to the right, and my decision was made. I stepped leftward, wondering how my father, the shopkeeper, and his father, the shopkeeper, had removed themselves from identical evil prospects.

There was one person I could ask. Mrs. Hemtobble had been misled by enthusiasm, but free of the veil of blood, her misjudgment was curable. As I walked to the Hemtobble place, I imagined myself falling to my knees, begging release from my musical vows. I brought the hoary black case to lay down before her like an unwanted baby. I was approaching the small, whitewashed house when I heard a violin.

It occurred to me that for all her work with me, I had never actually heard my teacher play. Listening now, I understood the fullness of her world in feir feir beat. I understood why she did not have any children, why she did not need them. She played the song of the Jews, of the remembered past and the redeemable future.

Come as a supplicant, I became an eavesdropper, standing on the porch, my eyes the height of the windowpane. Oh, the perversities of nature! That heavenly violin came from the same litter as my infernal match. It had the same amber coloring, the same bridge, fingerboard, and pegs; only its soul was different. It seemed to hover before her, attached by an invisible fifth string to the bulging Hemtobble chin. She was sitting in a chair, her bad foot stuck straight out like a boot, the other bent modestly inward. Her arm swept lazily back and forth.

Mr. Hemtobble lay flat on his back on the couch beside her. His mouth was open and a rheumy discharge seeped from his eyes. I could not tell whether he was awake, but his wife continued to play. The gently woven air seemed to soothe him.

It was beautiful, more beautiful than anything I could imagine, forget render, and it said to me: "You wretch. You ingrate. I give you the chance to perform this aching beauty, and you dare to refuse. With what, then, shall you fill the emptiness in your life?"

The melody, pitch, and meter varied, but the message remained, and I stood bound. Over the duration of the evening, however, the music grew langorous, exhausted. I thought that if I dozed off I would not be able to rise for a hundred years, and fought to keep my eyes open. I could see my instructor drooping perceptibly with every imaginary "Vun. Two." Then the sound, which had already faded, finally ceased. There was a silence full of presence. It was the quiet I had sought to give my parents. Mrs. Hemtobble was asleep in the formal position, her left elbow at rest on the arm of the chair, supporting both her unwieldy bulk and the violin. Mr. Hemtobble coughed and gestured helplessly, and the music resumed.

I played *The Spinning Song* that night as I had never played it before. Alone, in the dark, my stroke was more fluid, my fingers more nimble than lessons had taught me. I was attuned to the strains of the individual notes and the whole that contained them. For the elderly couple and my parents and the cat and all Proszowice, my brother, my cousins, my neighbors, and strangers, I persevered until dawn without a pause, without applause. I played the magical instrument the way my forebears had envisioned, but when I saw the first light it was time for me to retire.

I considered my parents' house. I could set the ancient violin back upon the shelf in the closet and progress with my studies as if nothing had happened. I could allow myself to succumb to the lures of my family's love, but I would never be better for them than I had already been, and I would never be as good for myself as I just was. The violin was simply not my instrument—except maybe for one night. Even sons can have moments of genius.

I no longer had the heart for dramatic revenge. Burning was too cruel a fate for the creator of beauty; neither would drowning or stoning do. I nevertheless walked toward the river, where I saw the hollow tree. I placed the violin—wood to wood, awaiting the prodigy of the future—into the narrow opening, into the hands of the sprites for safekeeping.

LeVitATION

From the end of summer until the High Holidays, there was always a great sense of expectancy about Proszowice. Once another season was complete, and harvest imminent, the prosperity of the farmers communicated itself to the merchants, who passed it along to the scholars, who spread it like loam on the fertile community ground. Amid the clamor of exchange, pyramids of ripe vegetables were transformed into cloth and herring and clocks. My mother cleaned our house from basement to beams and would have climbed up the chimney if my father had let her. To stop her, he took her by the arm to promenade in the square, "just because the air is so fine." Of course, most couples were not so enlightened, but these were people who considered sending their son to study in Cracow. They walked by the shul, where the sexton was riffling the pages of the prayerbooks to make sure that none had stuck together in the damp August heat. Everyone, in his or her own way, made ready for the New Year.

But I was impatient. I lived in an eternal now that would not conceive of either the soon or the later. I could not wait, and the pining burned my heart like a brand. Worse, though, I didn't know what it was I could not wait for. Come September, I would advance one grade in school and reach one shelf higher in my father's store. Maybe I would get more of the older boys' wit, but this was a minor accomplishment, and I craved the momentous. I was a self-conscious puppy with dreams of a mastiff. Sometimes, I felt so sheerly vital that I tugged my father out of bed to start the day. It was only during the first New Year's reading of the Shema Yisroael that I finally saw the form my inarticulate desire would take.

In the original days, the sons of Levi ministered to the needs of the priests, who were the sons of Aaron. With the destruction of the Temple and the dispersal of the Jewish people, these tribal roles disappeared, and along with them the defining characteristics of the tribes themselves. In Exile, there was no such thing as a Kohan or a Levite; there were only Jews. But on Rosh Hashanah, the descendants of the priestly caste performed one final act of sympathetic magic. Calling forth their vestigial powers, they blessed their brothers, not as men reciting holy writ, but as God's own dummies. So awesome was their metamorphosis that it was forbidden to look upon them during this ritual. To ensure that they would not even accidentally witness the Kohanim, some members of the congregation prayed with their backs turned.

Before these prayers could begin, however, the Kohanim had to be cleansed. They were helped, as of old, by the Levites, of whom my father, and therefore myself, were two. We met them at the water trough. I recognized their hands. Cohen the carpenter's were as rough as a piece of wood; his nephew Moscowitz's, only slightly less callous. Cohen the butcher's were tinged by the pink of the chickens whose heads he had so neatly severed for countless Friday night dinners. These were holy men?

"It is not Cohen, specifically," my father explained. "It is the office of his ancestors."

And were my ancestors any less fine than his?

"It is not a matter of better or worse. It is a difference without a value, a difference of function."

"I see," I said, seeing only that *I* had washed *their* hands.

Our heads were lowered so that only the Kohanim's feet and the fringes of the dipping prayer shawls were visible to us. My dissatisfaction increased through the preliminary chant. Moaning, keening, in thrall to an unseen God, their pains wracked the fragile sanctuary.

"You know why we really can't look," Jacob Lester nudged me. "That's because if you saw who was blessing you, you'd faint." Lester was our village cynic, though his eyes too were cast down. He was joking to ease the gravity of the occasion, but I felt the sting of truth.

And the Kohanim wept, "Hear, O Israel, the Lord our God, the Lord is One."

But why could Israel not see whence was imposed this limit? I cannot abide limits. I don't know when to stop. I have always, imagine that I always will, want to see or do whatever is pro-hibited—for precisely that reason.

The prayer of the Kohanim was drawing to a close. One more phrase and I would have been safe from the terrible annual temp-tation to peek. But one year more and I would be thirteen, a Bar Mitzvah, a man, responsible. I could not help but calculate this last fugitive opportunity and resolve to grab it. Decision, however, was easier than execution. My eyes seemed unable to obey my mind, as if there were coins taped to each lid. When I did finally yank them wide, I could have sworn that I heard the zloty clank to the temple floor, and I saw the unseeable—three old men. The Kohanim clutched their *tallisim* like tattered angels' wings.

It was the first deliberate act of religious disobedience of my life. I expected the slimy arm of the Devil to reach through the floor of the shul and drag me under.

I do not know what there was within me that made me so contrary. I do not know why I could not accept the lot drawn for me at birth and gratify my parents' and my people's expectations, so many of which I shared. I meant no disrespect, but I yearned for something they would never be able to understand. Right then, among my family and friends, beneath the lowering countenance of my God, "Blessed be the name of His glorious kingdom for ever and ever," I thought, "I want to fly."

Levitation has troubled the wise men for ages. Some have thought it a property of the real to be modified in accordance with established rules of nature. The air has a small but significant weight less than clouds, leaves, and yarmulkes. For more solid objects to join this category, change them. Transmute the elements. Others have denied that levitation is a matter of proportion. In order to achieve the literally transcendent, they wish to eliminate the very quality of weight while keeping those of blue or bitter. Reweave the fabric of being without that heavy thread, they say. Unfortu-nately, I treasured the God-given essences too much to consider tampering with one or removing another. Instead, I wished to add a new quality, that of levity, to those of substance. This may sound contradictory, but the true believer does not shrink from paradox: he embraces it.

Most physical laws have inspired similar philosophical quandaries. Invisibility, malleability, and magnetism have all undergone the deepest of Talmudic analysis, and each still has its advocates; but only weight, along with its airy antithesis, has spellbound men for so long. From the magician to the American technician, it has exercised the highest faculties of the human imagination.

But I wanted neither science nor the occult. I wanted merely to fly.

For the rest of the prayers my thoughts floated around my head like a halo. It is said that sometimes the Baal Shem Tov and his students became "so fired with learning that they knew not whether they were in Poland or in heaven." Some find this rapture in study, some in money, and some in love, but I found it in the images of flight that played on the periphery of my mind.

I could see the church spire off in the distance and, for a moment, I envied the cabbage heads their peak. They too did not know whether they were in Poland or heaven. I thought of Joshua, who stopped the sun; and I thought of Moses, begging for a sign of divinity, rapping the desert rock for water, subject to the sin of pride. God knows, I too was proud, but I was also reverent according to my own lights. My family would take my aspirations amiss, but, like them, I was in search of the presence of the holy. Only our maps differed.

Complete independence was the new first principle. My father, for example, did not stand or rely upon the floor; he bordered it. One's every motion was therefore a redefinition of the world. The Torah's silver crown pierced the firmament, while the twitch of my little toe shook the foundations. Yet look how delicately the pieces meshed! Wonderstruck by this drastic, immaculate configuring, I stood when those about me sat and sat when they stood and failed to notice the Rabbi's signal to his cantor. When the shofar blew its primitive cry, my cup overflowed. I saw my white knuckles and knew that if I let go of the dark wooden pew, I would rise with the ease of a balloon, until Zalman the Digger pulled my chin back to earth and said, "What are you, a statue?"

Just the opposite, I thought. They were the statues, caught fast beneath the millstones of their belief, unaware of the freedom that lay one step beyond. I may have looked like them, a Yiddish miniature in prayer shawl and yarmulke, but I was vibrating like a softly tapped cymbal. I felt a surge of power every time I considered what happened when I dared to behold the secret rites of the Kohanim—nothing, absolutely nothing. Ah, to shed the yoke that bore us down, to harness that magnificent lack, to meet the perfect contradictions of the Almighty on his own ground— that was my goal!

The prayers went on. We gave thanks and pled mercy for our sins, "sins committed knowingly or unknowingly, openly or secretly, under compulsion or freely . . . sins of scoffing, slander, impurity, presumption, and evil inclination . . . sins for which the law would have imposed chastisement, flagellation, excision, or one of the four death penalties," sins the mere enumeration of which would exhaust the most dedicated sinner.

Thoroughly convinced of the lowliness of our nature, we set off to Tashlikh. This is the one service conducted outside the synagogue proper, beside the nearest body of water, for in it we wash away our sins. We walked in contrite and motley procession (the Kohanim and Mrs. Horowitz and her three unmarried daughters, Mrs. Hemtobble leading her husband like a trained bear, Jergenchic the barber, Bobover, Kleiner, my father, my mother, my grandmother, my brother, my infant sister, and Zalman the Digger peering at the rest of us with the incuriosity he exhibited toward all who met him before their maker) from the shul through the question-mark-shaped streets of the town to the Proszowice River. This last was actually a sluggish irrigation ditch with muddy banks on which a few tenacious weeds had managed to entrench themselves. I felt the exhilarating dread of a soon-to-be martyr on the road to the gibbet or stake. There was heart-stopping fear and anxiety, but there was also a gratifying sense of curiosity contentable.

A spatter of shadows meant a flock of geese overhead. With the first shade of autumn in the tips of the leaves of the yew trees, they were traveling south from the Arctic Circle, maybe to Palestine. While I gazed idiotically after them—yearning, stumbling—the entire flock, as if acting on a single impulse or connected by invisible strings, banked steeply to the left, and alit by the river.

The geese had just settled into the shallows by the large hollow willow tree when we came upon them, a loud, homely mass; I was in the rear. There was a frightened, flapping, honking ruckus, and all except one of the geese rose, awkward until they cleared the willow and regained their impeccable V formation. In a twinkling they were dark stars in the distance, save the straggler. It pecked at a root not ten meters upstream, oblivious to both human presence and the absence of its mates.

The purification ceremony commenced. In most other villages the people threw bread into the water to represent the casting away of sins, but we washed; it was idiosyncratic. The men squatted and thrust their hands aggressively under the surface of the water, as if it were scalding. The women bent carefully, holding their dresses to their chests with one hand while letting the stream run over the other. Changing hands, they left soft, wet prints on themselves. A few of the youngest, most immature children were allowed to wade into the riverbed. I myself had done this five years before. Now, from the venerable antiquity of age twelve, I envied the little Mikovsky and the Balybys twins their freedom. After a day of solemn injunction and duty, the water beckoned with a sparkle I could not resist. I kicked off my shoes, peeled off my socks, and joined the babies, and everyone laughed.

Even the sole remaining goose turned its long, variegated neck to stare at me. Its eyes bulged. A thin, red-speckled snake was coiled around its leg. The snake slid down into the tidal muck, dragging the leg with it, and the goose fell off-balance. Its wings flapped and arched backward, and it called out to its bygone companions with a strident, pathetic honk.

The twins left the water.

There was a final thrashing of wings and a hoarse squawk as the graceful neck, limpid eyes, and tapering beak were pulled beneath the surface.

Several hands appeared to help me, but I was entranced by the last of the air bubbles and the few stray feathers that had begun to float downstream. It was then I realized that the time for my own personal ascent had finally come.

The prayers started, and I declared, *"Here,* O Israel."

I said to myself, on this site I shall willfully and without external aid levitate. My body, like bread, like breath, shall rise.

Let the Proszowicer laugh. I can hear their many mirthful tongues like voices in an orchestra. First is the din of the Rabbi and the Doctor's assertive trombone. Then comes an abundance of modestly chuckling clarinets: Jacob Lester, proud of his new shoes, Isaac the Millionaire, down-at-the-heels, Old Man Medisky smelling faintly of orchids. I can hear the stringy smirking of Reb Tellman, my teacher, and the lower, kindlier cellos of the other teachers I have known. They contrast with the mockery of the snare drums that are my classmates, from whom I am accustomed to such abuse. Finally, there is the ominous undertone of the bass multitude. They will not listen to the silent one until they realize that he is holding the baton. Let them laugh.

The only two who do not pass musical judgment are my father and my mother. They are worried, baffled as usual by their firstborn. In the meantime they smile with benign skepticism, and my mother reaches out gently to turn the pages of my prayerbook.

"Blessed be the name of His glorious kingdom for ever and ever." It is the third reading of those words today. Three times daily for the rest of the year they will be repeated, but never with the same clarity and passion. Graven in my mind like words on stone, they still leap skyward. I cry, "Amen!"

The congregation murmurs indulgently. Everyone in the world I know is standing on shore. They think I am daydreaming, but they are wrong. I am keenly aware of the lapping on the flesh beneath the hem of my short woolen pants. They are waiting for me to emerge. Instead, I stay in the water. I have always been a bit simple, they think. Pity the parents for the imbecile child, but I should know better. The joke has gone far enough. After all, this is Rosh Hashanah.

"And thou shalt love the Lord thy God with all thy heart, with all thy soul, and with all thy might." My voice climbs heroically.

My father whispers my name.

Someone glares at me, but he is complacent. Rich or wretchedly poor (predominantly the latter), the Jews of Poland have forgotten the gift and the glory we have been commanded to remember forever.

"Thou shalt teach them diligently unto thy children, speaking of them when thou sittest in thy house, when thou walkest by the way, when thou liest down, and"—here I tremble—"when thou risest up."

Reckoning on the progress of the text, I am nonetheless delighted when the words of the Shema echo my innermost ambitions. I am dressed in a white *tallis* that flutters in the autumn breeze as if it can hardly wait to bear me aloft. It has delicate blue embroidery and tassels that bounce merrily above the cool flow of the stream. A current eddies about the frail stalks that support me and begs to uplift me. Both air and water conspire to aid me. My act, however, must not be the accompaniment to prayer, for it is not illustration I seek, but revelation.

Somebody tugs at my tallis.

Remember, I am standing in the water, which is literally aswim with the cast-off sins of the previous year. Newly clean, the people hesitate to soil themselves again with their own impurity, of which each alone knows the secret extent. Only I am immune from this contamination, and will be until I emerge, which I reassure the Proszowicer I genuinely intend to do. The only thing is that, rather than step out of the running water, I plan to hover above it.

"Enough is enough," grumbles Old Man Medisky, whose greenhouse is as overgrown as his beard.

"He never knows when to stop," comments Isaac the Millionaire. This is true, but this time I don't have to. As long as I am out of their reach, I am within reach of my goal. A buoyant, ecstatic power enters the tips of my toes, rises through my feet, and stretches the muscles till my legs turn rubbery. Strange things happen at my center and then ride across the plane of my stomach. I thrust my arms upward, as if to grab ahold of the clouds.

"Hey!" they call in an attempt to break my reverie. There is a moment of surprise as they read the seriousness of my expression, and their humor fades.

"Do you have any idea what you're doing?" the Doctor asks.

"Answer him," Jacob Lester insists.

I smile blissfully, which turns their impatience to anger. The women's faces blanch, the men's turn red.

"Stop this immediately!" Reb Tellman commands, but I must answer to a higher authority. My teacher wears his orthodoxy like the crumpled gray hat that never leaves his head. Feast or famine, he bows to the superior wisdom of the Lord. I, too, bow, no questions asked, but I pray for an answer.

The Shema, the most beautiful of prayers, comes to a close.

"Ignore him," the Rabbi says. They think I want attention, that if they pretend I'm not there, I won't be. They stifle their laughter, and the prayers continue and not an eye deviates from the text to myself, still in the center of the moving stream. Together we recite the prayers, during which my intention becomes rock-solid. When the service is over, before we retire for dinner, my upraised arms stretch farther and creak. My knobby little knees quiver with the strain. I announce, "Hear *me,* O Israel."

And the Proszowicer freeze.

They cannot imagine this. It is as if they had seen the Kohanim. Until now my behavior has been outrageous, but this is obscene.

"Blessed be My entry to Your glorious kingdom for ever and ever."

The Rabbi is the one to break the spell. He blinks. His nostrils flare. His beard fairly bristles with fury. He proclaims it, "Sacrilege!"

And the Proszowicer erupt. Everyone at once—some to me, some to each other, some to themselves, some to God—are declaring, discussing, denying, "Shame!" Forbidden pagan doctrines and the most evil of practices are ascribed to me. From the depths of the crowd I hear the murmurous syllables, "Caballa."

Only my mother and my father remain quiet. It is their son, but what can they do? They will come with me if I rise, catch me if I fall.

My insides are churning. The power has seized my chest, inflamed my neck. It is a furnace that pumps hot air through the seared passages of my nose and throat, like a dragon. Steam obscures my vision; everything blurs into a translucent haze. Voices are raised in indistinguishable cacophony against the background of blue sky, blue stream—and a few dead feathers.

I begin to spin. I am like a Hanukkah top on the point of my toes, my arms flung out like wings for balance. Instead of slowing, however, I keep on gathering speed and momentum, pulling the water into a whirlpool around me. I feel that, through the sweat of my effort and centrifugal force, I am unloading the ballast of my worldly self into the disappearing funnel, along with the feathers. I am dizzy, nauseous, but I am laughing, splashing, and the surging power continues to stir me. "Amen!"

"Grab him!"

Both Rebecca the whore and Shivka Bellet—one in rhinestones, the other in pearls—are screaming, and the Rabbi is shaking his fist. Reb Tellman is trying to hook me like a fish. But without entering the stew of their past indiscretions these arms fall short into useless gestures of dismay on the bank.

I am on the verge, less connected with each revolution. Still I must spin faster, fast and faster than I possibly can, to achieve the holy thing, the name of which I must exalt myself to utter, "with all my heart, with all my soul, and with all my might . . . to levitate."

Mrs. Horowitz faints. Her legs are splayed like a cart horse that can no longer carry its weight. Her daughters try to revive her, to no avail. The Kohanim are wailing in tandem, beside whom Mrs. Hemtobble, Cohen the butcher's sister, the music teacher, taps her club foot.

"And you shall speak to me in the house. . . ."

The orchestra plays with a shattered vigor, drums pounding, brass blaring, violins screeching, so that they fail to notice that the pebbles rubbed smooth by the action of the stream are chattering like teeth in winter. The water is boiling and the individual rivulets that go to make up the mainstream seem to be twisting apart, like strings in an elaborate braid unwound, as I twist in the opposite direction, faster and faster.

"And by the way. . . ."

My head is filled with the rushing noise of the foot-deep stream, as if a dam had broken, as if Noah's deluge were pouring upon me from the infuriated heavens. The wind lashes at my tallis like waves. The waves rush through my toes like the wind.

"When I lie down. . . ."

I am a tree stripped bare by the ferocity of the storm and the searing sky waters, my hair and eyebrows plucked. My back is scored by invisible fingers tearing at me from the sanctified shore. Curses like salt shower into the wounds. The river is become hot tar, the clouds above me brimstone, but the fire feels good and the burning droplets etch through the last moorings that bind me.

"And when I rise up . . ."

Up.

I am lying on the ground. I can feel its rough, sandy surface against my cheek, and I can feel the air above me. I am nowhere near the river, but I am wet, drenched, a rag spread out in the yard to dry. I must blink several times to clear my vision of the muddy water and focus on the circle of concerned faces that surrounds me. They are no longer laughing, no longer angry. "Tell me," I croak. Don't we speak the same language?

I jerk myself into an upright position, but I no longer seem to have any strength. I am about to fall back when a familiar, reassuring hand becomes a pillar supporting the small of my back. I rub my cheek like a man touching his new beard. "Tell me," I beg.

"What?" my father asks.

"Anything you want," my mother answers.

"Did I . . . you know . . ." The sacred word is like a crystal on my tongue. I can't say it. "Lll. . . ?"

My mother sighs with the pain.

My father says, "We don't know."

Don't they have eyes?

He explains. Men were shouting, women screaming, children sobbing. I was jumping and splashing, and the sky turned black. Looking into the heart of a fountain, who can say if the marble figure moves? I fell, maybe slipped on one of the chattering stones. My father, ever the Levite in aid of the holy, saved me from the river of sin.

That poised on the brink of flight I should have been subject to accident is ludicrous. I had been empty of myself and filled with the majesty, I was certain, to rise. All I wanted between myself and the world was the height of a grain of sand, the depth of a drop of water. But if the Devil was not strong enough to stop me from gazing at the Kohanim, if the Kohanim were not strong enough to effect their magic, if God himself was not strong enough . . . why should I be different?

Maybe I was different. Maybe the sight of the Proszowicer was veiled by the grandeur of my ascent. Why, then, is memory gone?

My father and my mother look at me with the inexpressible ignorance born of love and the rending knowledge that there is nothing we can do to help each other.

The

Apprentice

*H*unger is in the stomach of the beholder.

The fast of Yom Kippur was nearly here. Years past and years future were the twin arms of a scale, with the tentative present the point upon which they balanced. One sin too many and the past would tender its grim embrace. One good deed might inaugurate a future. The Jews of Proszowice examined their souls like the nobility did their faces in the anteroom to the king's chambers: Is that wrinkle caused by idle gossip? Is that blemish due to pride? As soon as the shofar blew to herald the New Year, we could see the spiritual crow's-feet we all bore with unusual clarity. Isaac the Millionaire gave alms, Bobover ate kosher, and the Rabbi tormented himself with doubts about his faith. Still, Isaac continued to scheme, Bobover to sell rotten vegetables for fresh, and the Rabbi to conduct services. As my father said, "A man has to eat."

Hunger, however, is in the stomach of the beholder. And the merest though of the approaching fast was intolerable to me. Earlier that afternoon, Reb Tellman had rapped my knuckles for eating in class. Then, because my fingers were swollen, I dropped my prayer book and he smacked me again. The other students dubbed me "Buttercookiefingers." But neither my teacher's nor my fellows' insults hurt me as much as the ill will of God, blessed be the Master of the Universe.

My father smiled broadly. "Hello. How was school?"

I shrugged. "Fine." I began to sleepwalk through the store toward my homework. I recalled a caterpillar I had once watched crawling up the side of a porch. Its many legs wiggled and its back arched with the effort. After fifteen minutes it finally reached the wooden plateau, and I flicked it off onto the grass. I was being punished in kind for the sin of my presumption.

"Hey, dreamer, . . . anything new?"

I struggled to decipher the hidden meaning. How could I play such a game at a time like this. New? Yes, the roots of trees untied my shoes. "No."

He seemed disappointed. "Don't you notice anything different?" His arms spread wide to comprehend his kingdom. I was obliged to scan the familiar shelves, from which dozens of bolts of cloth protruded like multicolored gun barrels beneath rows of hammers and saws and gauged, notched, geared tools, and, especially, food. We sold material because my great-grandfather had sold material, and we sold hardware because my grandfather had sold that, but mostly we sold food because my father's first love was edibles. As the satin and screwdrivers of previous generations gradually disappeared, he refilled the shelves with wide-necked bottles of jelly and marmalade and tins of imported mustard. But those were items that anybody could order, stock, and sell. The "perishables" required more skill in the keeping. There were cheeses—yellow and orange, crusty, runny, ripe, and pungent—and dried figs, apricots, and glazed pears. There were barrels of pickles—sour, half-sour, and dill—and nuts of a dozen different varieties in open-topped canisters, and coffees, whose exotic aromas seeped through their containers' lids. There was chocolate in hunks like iron ore and hard candy like jewels.

The pride of the store was the fish: sleek herring in brine or cream sauce, whole or deboned, salmon smoked to fleshy pink perfection, sable, sturgeon, and white fish, their opaque eyes staring like marbles through the display case. That was it!

Six feet long, two wide, and a foot and a half deep, a gleaming glass box outlined in oak, the new case stood on elegantly carved legs that tapered down to ball-and-claw feet. It had been ordered eons before from a glazier in Cracow. At first we were surprised that it took so long. Then we were angry, then resigned, until the matter became a family joke. If my mother wanted to put me off she would say, "You can stay up till ten when the new display case arrives." Like the Messiah, it had to come—eventually. Now, here it was. My father fairly beamed with pride. He was laying fish down on a bed of shaved ice as carefully as a nurse a newborn. Already the glass was misted with what I imagined to be the last gasps of the expiring salmon. I was turning my father's celebration into a funeral.

"Come, help me," he said, offering a gift to his eldest son. It was not just anybody he would allow to polish his treasure. I took the rag and set to wiping the clouds from the coffin. Its beveled edges formed a glass prism. When shined and lit, it cast a rainbow that made the ice inside look like diamonds. That was the first moment I truly felt hunger.

The store was actually the front parlor of our house. Behind a curtained archway were the kitchen and the stairs to the bedrooms. Naturally, when business was slow, which was often, my father sat reading in the kitchen, beside my mother, who was cooking. At the end of a chapter he would stand up, stretch, taste the borscht, and say, "More salt, I think."

Between his fish and her ever-bubbling soups and stews, it was a miracle that I wasn't as plump as a partridge. I was, in fact, lean. My veins stood out like tattoos on my skinny arms. My knees and elbows and all my joints were bony, my motions consequently marionettish. My pointy fingers were always engaged with strings, rubber bands, pencils, and cookies.

"Can't sit still, eh?" the barber remarked as I squirmed in his red leather throne.

"I don't think he knows how," my father said.

Jergenchic was our local man of science. He nodded sagely while stropping his razor and said, "It's his metabolism."

Like the stray dog who occupied our backyard, I was never full. My mother would click her tongue with pity and throw the dog a bone. He would gnaw it to splinters, bury it, then beg for more. When my father and I set out to smoke the latest shipment of fish, he followed us at a slavering trot.

The slabs of raw fish were laid on a large grill that took up nearly all the space in the little stone hut. Underneath the grill were two feet of birch sawdust on top of which my father spread strips of packing cardboard and a few dozen nuggets of coal. The paper would ignite the coal, which would bring the sawdust base to a slow burn, which would cook, dry, and preserve the fish. My father dug into his vest pocket for a match.

We stepped back from the intensity of the heat. Suddenly I understood the first principle of existence. From God's tears, which fed the ocean, to the fish that lived there until they were caught and brought, smoked, to our breakfast table, food was the basic stuff of life. Eating was the basic activity, hunger the basic condition. A man has to eat. It's his metabolism.

My family was in the kitchen, the morning sun slanting past a row of tomatoes ripening on the sill. Four places were set at the table, one each for myself and my brother, my father, and my grandmother. My sister never left her cradle. My mother would eat later. She dealt out plates like playing cards. There were bottles of milk and juice and a dish of butter, and two blue ceramic dishes of sugar and salt. Eggs were boiling on the stove, bread baking inside it.

My brother was impatient. He whispered and giggled and drummed the table with his utensils. He dangled a shoelace over my baby sister, hoping that she would reach for it like a cat. Instead, my grandmother snatched the cord. She was incredibly quick for an old lady. My father's head was buried deep inside Genesis. My mother was everywhere, pouring, mixing, wiping my sister's mouth, patting my grandmother's head, practically turning the pages in my father's book.

"Thank you," he muttered.

"Sleep well?" she asked me.

That was an odd question. I always slept well. Given half a chance now, I would turn around, climb the stairs, and close my eyes for another day. Wrapped in my quilt like a cocoon, I could float like a hummingbird, swim like a trout. Sleep well? I should say so!

"Pfeh." It sounded like my brother was spitting.

"What's that?"

"I always go 'pfeh' when something doesn't agree with me."

Food came: a platter of fish, the eggs, the bread to be sliced and spread. We were as frugal as the next family, cold in the winter, ill-clad and unkempt, but in Proszowice the cobbler's children always had shoes, and we never went without food. Nevertheless, I felt as if the Yom Kippur fast, still twenty hours away, was already upon me. I was starved.

"We learned a new chapter of the Bible yesterday," my brother said. "Jonah."

"Tell us." My father encouraged him.

I had made the same recitation myself at his age. No doubt my father carried memories of a similar performance at his father's table. No doubt it was the same table, its burns, stains, and defacements an enduring history of our family's domestic life.

I heaped my plate with enough food to cover the surface, then I dug in.

"But why," my father inquired, "did the whale swallow Jonah?"

"I don't understand the question."

"You keep explaining why Jonah was eaten, but you ignore the whale's motive. It is a matter of perspective."

Distracted by the munchings and gulpings that punctuated my father's theology, I lost my place in his dialogue. I could not maintain perspective when all I felt was the itch to eat and keep eating. I refilled my plate.

"I know," my brother said. "Because it was the will of God."

"Maybe," I said, "the whale was hungry."

"Pfeh."

"What's the matter with you, you sniff at everything I say."

"Now, boys."

"I'll give him a 'pfeh' he'll remember."

We rose glaring, then, grappling, fell back locked in brotherly struggle. A can of juice tilted and toppled in a stream of yellow. Our baby sister began to squall, our grandmother to pluck imaginary stars out of the kitchen sky.

"Hey, hey!" My father pried us apart. "What's wrong with the two of you? Can't you sit at a table for a single meal without going at each other's throats?"

"How can I get at his throat when he's always eating?"

I hadn't known he had noticed. There was usually a filbert on the way from my pocket to my mouth, often a macaroon crumbling within me, not to mention regular meals plus sandwiches of leftovers spread on half a challah roll, smeared with fat. The only time I wasn't eating was when I was sleeping. I stuck out my tongue. "Pfeh."

Baited, he bit. "And you thought you were being so secretive, but you kept me awake all night going back and forth to the icebox. I'll bet there're still chicken bones in your bed."

It was as if he had struck me. I knew it was true. I hadn't remembered until he said it, but I could feel the carpet pricking my sleepwalking feet, the banister in my cupped palm. I could see the moonlight glow, touch the midnight cold. I could almost taste my somnambulist snack.

"So he ate at night. A man has to eat. So big deal, so everybody's even, so I don't want trouble between my sons."

We settled into a resentful truce. Only my baby sister ignored the general edict. She was ugly and unhappy, yet the adults were thrilled by everything about her. I wished that I could kick and scream and have people come to spoon-feed me. Yes, I was jealous of the disgusting milky farina that she spilled onto her miniature chin. Food was the God-given pacifier for everyone except me, the merest thought of which it inflamed.

Listening to the clacking of my grandmother's toothless gums and my father's meditative chew, I regretted my outburst, and I think my brother felt the same. Neither of us wanted to turn our parents' home into a battleground, but we were temperamental, subject to inspiration, dejection, love, and fury. It was our metabolism. In the spirit of the season, I felt like asking forgiveness, but the words of contrition stuck in my throat like lumps of porridge. Perhaps I did not want pardon, either human or divine. The very idea of Yom Kippur, its fast and purgation, made my belly ache with distress.

As if he could read my mind, my brother said, "Well, you better not, because even if I don't see you, God will."

"Hush now," my mother said. "I think God can take care of his own business, young man."

It was my brother's turn to stick out his tongue.

All in all, it was a typical morning. I began to gather my books and papers for school, and to pack my lunch with special interest. I mumbled goodbye and passed through the curtained archway into the store.

The day before, a package of jellied chestnuts had arrived. I could practically smell the sweet amber juice through the ornamental jar. I decided to try one. Swollen, the chestnut was barely smaller than my mouth, in which it burst with a fabulous, fruity savor. My metabolism ran as wild as a thermometer plunged into boiling water. Chewing deliriously, I happened to look up. Through the dusty film of the window I saw a Pole, a beggar, Dominick Verschtal by name.

He was a frightful man who used to work in the stables, where he maltreated the animals in his care. One horse in particular aroused his enmity, Alaska, a splendid bay mare, the property of H. D. Bellet. Dominick had waited for a morning Alaska was late in rising to whip the sleepy mare. She reared and kicked him. Although his face was split into ugly, uneven halves united by a bloody seam, he stood and lashed the proud creature to death. Bearing the shameful mark of the dead horse's hoof, he was fired and turned to begging.

Now he glared at the golden juice dribbling down my chin with an expression of such pure hatred that I lowered my eyes. I saw the chestnuts. I could not resist. I ate the entire batch as if they were raisins. When I finally felt the clot in my stomach, I had the bizarre conception that I was pregnant. With what, a tree? Worst of all, I was still unsated.

The high holidays were a good season for our business, which did not rely on everyday consumption. People bought appetizing for Shabbos morning or a zloty's-worth of candy for their children or chocolate for their sweethearts. These were special morsels for special moments, none of which rivaled the first meal after Yom Kippur. Everyone would want to break their fast with the best food they could afford. The new display case had arrived just in time.

Every day thereafter I saw my father standing behind his case, like a judge on a bench. He pointed out to customers the beveled edges and brass fittings, the clever way the hinges worked and the fine workmanship of the carpenter: "Look, here on the side, it's a leaf. Looks so real makes you want to pluck it." Word spread quickly, and within three days half of the community had been in to ooh and ahh. Hours from anywhere, this was big news. The Rabbi pronounced a blessing and accepted a half-pound of lox in return.

A queue formed.

"And maybe a quarter-pound of the sturgeon," Mrs. Hemtobble ordered.

I was helping out after school. It was a double spectacle for the customers, the new case tended by the prodigal child. "Yes'm." I humbly whetted the knife.

"Is it goot?"

"Oh, yes'm."

"Maybe I could have a taste?"

Customers were not allowed free samples. That was the rule, observed only as an exception; bargains made customers happy. But this week there was not even a pretense of reluctance in the giving. My father knew that the new case endowed the fish with an extra, salty tang, and since it was a special occasion Mrs. Hemtobble conceded, "So make it a half-pound. And talk of extravagant, did you hear that Skivka Bellet has pledged a new pew for the shul?"

"*I* will donate the same," Isaac the Millionaire said, picking from his teeth his fourth sample of the day, about to try a fifth. It was the thought that counted.

Zalman the Digger, in for a new crowbar, the last of my grandfather's supply, said that *his* were the only seats that were certain to be filled.

"Morbitt!" Mrs. Hemtobble commented. "So where's my three-quarters pound?"

"Coming right up, Ma'am," I took the fish by the tail, sliced off the thin, translucent layers, weighed it, wrapped it in wax paper, and opened the drawer to take the money.

The problem here was that each time I handed a bagful of sturgeon or creamed herring with onions over the new display case my mouth watered. I wanted to grab the bag back and crawl into a hole to devour my outlaw's prey. Luckily, I subdued these urges. "Why bother?" I asked myself. I knew the well was bottomless.

My father pushed through the curtain after me. He could see that something was wrong. He kept a careful eye on me as we stacked newly arrived goods or strung them festively from the rafters or pyramided them in the aisles so that my friend Moshele Rosen could harass me by asking for the base can. It wasn't the repiling that bothered me but the temptation. The more food I saw, the more I craved.

My father had something to say, but didn't know how to say it. He paced uncomfortably and let his fingers run along the edge of the glass. "You know," he began, "you're not a Bar Mitzvah yet. I mean, well, you don't have to fast if you don't want to."

Hunger scratched at my stomach walls, but I knew that no food could fill me. I was parched, but knew that no liquid could slake my thirst. I was unslakeable. It was my metabolism. "No, thank you."

My mother slipped unobtrusively into the room. Her eyes were large with dark circles underneath them. "You're a growing boy," she said.

How could I explain that only by withstanding the urge might I overcome it, that eating was a vulgar habit anyway. And wasn't Yom Kippur about purification through starvation? Everyone over thirteen was forbidden to eat or drink, even a drop of one's own blood. I would show the God who decreed this that I could not only endure but surpass his dictum. I replied, "I prefer to join you." Come hell or high water, I would break the metabolic hold on me. A man does *not* have to eat.

Forget the headless chickens strung by their bony feet. Forget the heaps of sweet potatoes crowding the market stalls. Forget even the lox and chocolates of my father's store. For Yom Kippur the earth itself fed the fires that sustained the air that fed the waters that nourished the earth in an endless, voracious round. There was no escaping from the first principle. If I shut my eyes, my nose grew with the odor to anti-Semitic proportions. Stuff the nose, I could hear vegetables cry. Plug the ears, I could *feel* the world of food surrounding me.

Yom Kippur was the Day of Judgment, but when I woke that morning I was sure that my soul was already in the ever-burning kitchens of damnation. A day without food was my idea of forever.

My brother was pacing as if the prohibition on eating also applied to sitting. My father made a show of perusing the Book of Laws but cast wistful glances in the direction of the herring. My mother, helped by my grandmother, was working feverishly to prepare the evening's fast-breaking meal. It would be a gorger's delight, strips of fish and cheese laid out around a loaf of pumpernickel bread like the rays of a dark sun. There were berries for dessert.

In Palestine, I had heard, parts of the desert were baked so hard by drought that when it did rain, once a decade, the ground could not absorb it. The water poured off a thousand square miles of blasted rock, building up speed, gathering strength in the wadis, converging furiously on the lowest spot of the planet, the Dead Sea. The reason we know about these flash floods is that sometimes there are biblical archaeologists digging nearby. Any caught in the torrent's path are found the next day drowned, drowned in the middle of the desert, with not a drop of water for miles.

"Try not to think of it," my father advised.

"Think of what?" I answered. "I'm not hungry."

"Pfeh."

"Hurry or we'll be late for synagogue." This was my mother, hoping to stave off another confrontation.

She needn't have worried. I was too weak to fight, in a foggy delirium of hunger. "I don't mind," I said. "But I'd like to stay here a while longer . . . I'll catch up with you."

The doorbell jingled as my family went out. I walked around the kitchen and stretched in the silence. Without a mother, a grandmother, and at least one other sibling sharing the floor, the room was enormous.

"Temple," I thought. "It is no accident that temple and temptation have the same linguistic root." I would sit beside my father at the rear of the sanctuary. I would imitate his movements throughout the devotion, and somehow the correct words would issue from my ravenous mouth. "Who shall live and who shall die? Who shall be wealthy and who shall be poor?" These were the alternatives posed to the Lord of Hosts on this, the holiest day of the year. "Who shall be tranquil and who shall be afflicted? Who shall eat . . . "

I staggered from the kitchen, entangling myself in the archway's curtain, crashing into a ziggurat of marzipan. When I came up against the new display case, I gazed blearily through the glass at the gaping fish and the heavenly ice like diamonds. I felt observed. Maybe it was my imagination.

I was hungrier than I had ever been in my life. I could have eaten all of the fish, swallowed the ocean they once swam in. The metal-gray herring winked, the creamy white sturgeon beckoned. The delicate pink of the smoked salmon was the dawn of a new day. It seemed that if I could only take one single bite, I could finally satisfy myself. The display case opened without a creak. I lifted a butterfish that looked as if it had been gold-plated.

The doorbell rang.

I thrust the fish into my pocket, afraid that it was the Rabbi or Reb Tellman or the Angel of Death come with his flaming sword to haul me to justice. I wanted to jump behind the beautiful glass to hide.

It was Dominick Verschtal. Few Poles ever came into our store, Dominick never, but he looked around as if it were as familiar to him as Veselka's Tavern. He ambled up to the new display case, tapping it with a garish steel ring he wore by a knuckle, and said, "Well, pardon me if I didn't think that this was a Yiddisha home."

"We're not open."

"Tell it to the door."

I gripped the case with both hands. "May I help you?"

He squinted and grinned in such a way that his face rippled over the scar Alaska had left him. "Ye-e-s, ye-e-s you may," he said. "What can you recommend?"

I suggested, "Perhaps a little sable?"

"Hmm."

"Or maybe you'd like the whitefish?"

He growled.

My eyes flickered down to the lox, which lay stripped before me. Of course there was no religious sanction, but the thought of this horse-killer eating my father's pride seemed unholy.

"May I have a taste?"

"We don't usually. . . . "

"But after all, it is a holiday," he smirked.

"Here." I cut a sliver of the red flesh and handed it to him on the edge of the blade.

His lips smacked loudly. "I can't really get a solid taste. May I have some more?"

I was too frightened to refuse. I hoped he would take what he wanted and leave. I gave him another, then another slice, the glutton, and for the first time since my unnatural cravings had begun, they began to abate. Maybe it was fear, maybe humiliation, but maybe the Lord of Hosts, blessed be His name, was kind. With each piece of lox Dominick ate, the scales of hunger tilted farther from me. The fish's spine grew more prominent, like the spine of a starving child, as I automatically sliced and handed, sliced and handed, with insane politeness. "Another, sir?"

His answer came from deep within the stuffed gut. "No-o-o." He looked at me. "I think I'm full. Besides if you Jews can fast all day, I can hold off until dinner. I know when to stop."

"And will you be purchasing anything today?"

He laughed and said, "There's nothing here to buy."

I looked down with horror at the lox skeleton enlivened only by clinging shreds of red fish flesh. A week's profits were gone, but along with them went my appetite, thank God.

"Typical Jew!" Dominick sneered. "On this holy day, he tries to sell bad goods. I ought to. . . . " He lifted the back of his hand as if to strike me, but I stood my ground, and the hand with the ring came down on top of the beautiful display case—and a line like a lightning bolt appeared in the glass. Then Dominick strolled back through the jingling front door, dropping a handful of peanuts into his mouth.

I felt along the top of the case, but it was smooth. I reached inside, beside the carcass of the lox, and it was smooth there too. The crack was embedded in the glass. I rubbed and rubbed, hoping to rub the flaw out, but it was useless.

I looked up through the strings of dried mushrooms hanging from the rafters and thought that this was what I had been destined to learn here, working with my father: not how to slice and sell dead fish, but how to contain my hunger.

I was about to close the lid of the display case when I remembered the butterfish in my pocket. I set it down reverently in its larger cousin's place and tucked it in with a small heap of diamondlike ice chips. There would have to be an explanation later. The important thing was that after the fast I would no longer be hungry. Then, maybe, I could eat.

The Quilt and

the Bicycle

My quilt was a bag of sleep. Tucked under it like the jelly in a blintz, I was immune to the frost on the window. Neither chill nor disease could penetrate the patchwork; nor could fear, disillusionment, or dismay. I was protected from Cossacks, Tatars, Mongols, and Turks. Beneath my quilt, I was safe.

It was corduroy and cotton, wool, chenille, and one square of bright satin. It was beige with red flowers and green streaks and a yellow star and menorahs and bunnies and trains. In short, it was like every other quilt in Proszowice, but it was mine—mine before I knew the meaning of ownership, mine before I knew the nature of selfhood, my first possession.

Whenever a woman was expecting to become a mother, the other women sent their congratulations in fabric. Each donated one swatch and a few zloties for their joining. The red satin, for example, was the gift of the dowager Shivka Bellet, while the less ostentatious women brought plainer textiles in modest pastels. The Rebbitsin always gave bunnies.

Mr. Itzkowitz, the quilt master, sewed the patches into an elaborate cloth mosaic, which he stuffed with the down of a hundred Polish geese. Though composed of identical elements, no two of his patterns were the same; chosen at random, intuition lent them grace. And when the last stitch was knotted, Mr. Itzkowitz presented the art of his labor at the crib of the new human being. It was shield and succor wrapped into one, wrapped around one, a second skin. Bearing infant stains, adolescent scars, patches on the patches, bald spots, and other marks of age, a quilt more often than not traveled a lifetime with its owner. On her marriage day, a young woman's quilt was borne from her parents' house to her husband's, held at the four corners by the in-laws. Its top half was sewn to the bottom of the groom's to symbolize their union. Sometimes people requested that their quilts be rent at their death, and the feathers would flutter over the open grave like lost souls. Sometimes a quilt was used as a shroud.

In the morning, it was difficult to crawl out from under the comforting heap. My muscles were utterly at rest, my mind at ease, but school and the store and my familial responsibilities beckoned in the breakfast hubbub. I rolled free, and the bed lay virgin. Exposed now, I shivered into my pants, shrugged on suspenders, quickly prayed, and put on the shoes that peeked out from under the mattress frame. I splashed ice water on my groggy face and let the steam of the oatmeal thaw me.

Off to school, I saw Mr. Itzkowitz through the window of his shop. He worked in the middle of a perpetual storm, like a miniature Alpine guide in a paperweight, except instead of a scarf he wore a gauze mask over his mouth to keep from inhaling the feathers. I imagined that his wife plucked him clean every night.

My brother pinched me. "You! Daydreamer," he said. "We have to hurry."

Picturing Mr. Itzkowitz melting like a snowman, I rushed past the row of shops to the tiny schoolyard. My athletic peers were kicking a soccer ball back and forth while the intellectuals were engrossed in their books. Moshele Rosen was the center of some attention, talking fast, jabbing the air, apparently running in place. I could sense the skepticism in the circle around him before I could see Moshele's own face, full of beleaguered sincerity. He was saying: "So don't believe me. It was an enormous metal insect."

Moshele may have had his faults, but they were those of exuberance rather than guile. I knew for a fact that he did not lie—because I did—but that's another story. Accustomed to doubt, I could recognize the voice of truth. The best way to get Moshele to reveal something, however, was to pretend that you didn't care to hear it.

"So did this insect sting you?" I laughed.

"Don't be silly. A boy was riding it."

"Like a horse, I suppose?"

"Except it was much thinner . . . you could see the bones."

Reb Tellman appeared in the doorway like a shadow. He took his watch from his pocket, as if to say, "Heaven help the lad who dares to be late for my class," and we all filed inside.

The subject of the day was the Babylonian exile. Trapped behind the warped oak table with a despot for a teacher, I understood the plight of the old Jews better than anyone could imagine. I was gazing out of the classroom's one window, pondering the expanse of Kastel Street, when an apparition occurred. Unexpected, it nearly went undetected. I caught it like a well-kicked soccer ball, not by sight but by a goalie's unerring reflex. It was the glamorous metal insect, exactly as described, and, yes, there was a thin young man atop it, his jacket billowing out behind him like a butterfly's wings. The sash blocked them abruptly from view.

To engrave the fleeting image on my mind, I drew a picture: twin circles connected by an intricacy resembling a cloven timepiece. Silly Moshele, it was a machine, and I fancied myself as its inventor as I attached this spoke to that hub, that gear to this chain, the wheels to the curved horns which steered them. Unfortunately, my lines bore no relation whatsoever to the practical reality of either the object or the moment. Reb Tellman's ruler slammed down on my unsuspecting finger, and the sketch went flying.

"That's it!" Moshele whispered—to his regret, as the ruler found its second knuckled target.

"That's what?" Reb Tellman scoffed, looking down at the strange diagram. "A broken pair of glasses?"

Later I showed the blueprint to my parents. So it wasn't an engineer's ideal: I could recognize it and Moshele could too. "Yes, I've heard of such things, in Warsaw perhaps," my father said, then sank back into the Talmudic analysis of fish. "Reb Yossuf says that scales may be likened unto worldly goods. Their sparkle is of little account when the fish dies, but their waves have repercussions forever."

"How nice, dear," my mother said, tasting the soup, and I didn't know whether it was my father or myself she was addressing. To her, fish and the future were topics of equal import.

Whatever the tricks of fate, my immediate future was awfully predictable. Lying in bed, contemplatively naked beneath the bedsheets, I named the red dot inside a square of white wool

"Proszowice." I imagined the parallel lines in the next square to be the main roads to Cracow, which was the paisley flower in the square beyond. I situated Warsaw, Paris, and, on the far side of a strip of blue, the United States of America. Disguised as my fingers, the insect machine took me on a journey over the water, over the mountains, up and down the peaks and valleys I made with my knees. Only the sky was verboten. I had learned my lesson, and now, in lieu of mystery, I had found technology. I had seen the fabulous transport with my own eyes, drawn it truly. Still, it was rejected by the petty, provincial world in which I lived. The sole niche for this glory was my patchwork sanctuary. Safely beneath the plush comfort of my quilt, I dreamed of bicycles.

"Come! Quickly! Inside!" My mother stood sentinel at the front door, like every other mother in Proszowice that particular afternoon. It was a gauntlet of mothers we passed through, each verbally paddling us homeward, each grabbing her offspring, slamming and bolting doors behind them. "Thank God you're here!"

"I'm always here. I want to go out and play."

"Not today," she said. "The gypsies are in town."

I thought of the boy on the bicycle. He had had a face the color of coffee surrounded by waves of dark hair like a girl's.

They were camped on the outskirts of the village. Nobody ever saw them, but everybody knew where they were. We tantalized each other with tales of stolen children and chickens' heads. They prayed to the moon in black-magic pagan rituals and indulged in further depravities over which married people only were permitted to giggle and tsk tsk. Then the rumors began to acquire an uncomfortable tangibility. Rebecca the whore appeared at the café in a lustrous black and red gypsy shawl, the sight of which lingered in my mind like perfume. "Well what else could you expect of such a creature?" the other women buzzed, and gushed, "How lovely!" when the eminently respectable Shivka Bellet wore a bracelet in the shape of a snake swallowing its own tail. Then Moshele

Rosen was caught with a pocketknife. Reb Tellman smacked him and confiscated the weapon, but the influence was too pervasive to halt. It advanced like a fog.

Most of the other kids wanted to know about the carved handle and the temper of the blade.

"I suppose you found it in the street," I said.

"The market."

"At the stroke of midnight maybe?"

"Early morning."

"Thank you," I said, smiled, and felt my heart sink. Armed with knowledge of the where and the when, the how loomed insurmountably. Shivka Bellet was the richest woman in town, Moshele's father was a furrier, and everyone knew about Rebecca. Given a zloty a week's allowance, I had faint chance of more than a glimpse of the holy object.

The gypsy boy and his bicycle leaned against the pedestal of the statue of Otto IV. Up close, he was even darker than from a distance. His eyes were as black as his hair, which was bound in a leather thong. He was dressed in rags, but he wore them with an air of impoverished grandeur, and probably had another knife up his threadbare sleeve. He made no sign of recognition as I approached, then his hand opened. In it was a brooch of beaten silver sparkling with rubies.

I shook my head, and the brooch disappeared. He observed me in a sullen, imperial manner. I pointed to the bicycle, and he shook his head.

That night there was a frost. Branches snapped off and froze into thorns that pierced my thin-soled boots as I walked to school next day. Huddled against the wind, I pushed forward for the sake of eternal wisdom when all I truly desired was a moment of warmth. My lips cracked, my voice broke into a petulant whine. I could see the rimy patterns on Mr. Itzkowitz's window, and I wished I could crawl in between the stitches of his slumberous accommodation. It was a perfect day to stay in bed.

One result of the sudden frost was the cluster of local farmers surrounding the statue of Otto IV as if it were a campfire. The cart beside the bicycle within the cluster was heaped with vegetables and potatoes that would go bad in another day. The brooch, on sale for the price of ten kilos of potatoes, was traded directly for twenty-five kilos. Despite his good fortune, the boy still wore the same tatterdemalion outfit he had the day before. I could see his skin puckering with the cold. His shiver went down my spine in a sympathetic seizure, and I knew what I could offer him.

The ridges of the corduroy, the nub of the wools, the sleekness of the satin were like worms wriggling over my flesh. I could hear them in the rustling of the down. I could smell them—or was that the aroma of noodle pudding snuck into bed, books read by tallow candles, and my own unwashed body? It was not merely a quilt but my entire past that pressed down upon me—the weight of armor, the flimsiness of paper. In spite of the cold I was warm; but in spite of the comfort, I could not sleep. I knew the anguish of the insomniac. I tossed and turned and wondered how I had ever been able to sleep in such a pitiful, wrinkled bag of guts, and the further I burrowed into the folds, the more impossible it was to relax. Before I knew it, my mother tiptoed in.

"Up so early?" she cooed.

"It's my turn to clean the cheder. I have to be there first." I calmed her fears for my safety by saying that a friend was to meet me in the square.

"Who?" she began, when, as usual, my baby sister woke the rooster. In the ensuing tumult, I packed the quilt into an unwieldy mass and rushed off without saying goodbye.

My appointment was late. He didn't know it, but I stood in a doorway by the market's entrance waiting for him, counting the seconds. If he didn't arrive soon I would have to lug my bedding to school. I could imagine Reb Tellman's response, a rhythmic tapping of his ruler, a click-click-click that changed into the welcome pulse of two-wheeled traffic. I stepped to block his path, a one-man border guard with a bulging armful of fabric and feathers. He rode wide as if to evade me, then curved back in an arc and stopped dead sideways in front of me. I threw the quilt to the pavement.

The gypsy boy could not tell whether this was a greeting or a challenge. Breathing great puffs of vapor through a nose as wet as a puppy's, he stood his ground with aggressive pendency.

"Excuse me," I said.

He did not speak Yiddish.

I pointed to the quilt and to the bicycle and made gestures of exchange. He nodded uncomprehendingly until he began to understand. Then his head stopped moving and his eyes opened. This dawning of specific knowledge was a thing to behold, and I wondered if Reb Tellman had ever felt the privilege. After the dawn, however, came the storm. The gypsy shook his head vehemently, made a fist, and jabbered at me. Now maybe I was lucky that my mother tongue was my only tongue, because I heard a wistful tone that belied the obvious meaning of his words. Probably it was his accent.

"Come now, you don't really mean that, do you?"

He stamped his foot and got ready to pedal off, yet the bicycle remained steadfast. I picked up the quilt and placed it on his shoulders like a chamberlain adjusting his majesty's cloak. The waif/king bucked—or tried to, or pretended to—ineffectually, and I could feel the icicles in his neck melting. He looked amazed as his shoulders hunched farther into the downy checkerboard, and he hugged it, and the puckers left his knees, and he ceased to puff steam. The wetness dried under his nose and welled in his eyes. He stepped off his throne and gravely gave me the scepter and orb. "Handlebars," he called them.

My schoolmates scattered before me like chickens before a team of eight. Knees aquiver, stomach churning, my hands jerking the machine from left to right to maintain a fitful balance, I rode among them with the solitary omnipotence of a cavalryman amid the mass. My fleeing prey could not tell that my mount was absolutely out of control; they were too busy evading its every surprising wobble. This was far from the effortless glide I had expected—unreasonably, I admit. Even swans have paddles. Even a rolling stone must be set in motion; besides which, starting was no longer a problem. Starting was easy; stopping, another matter entirely. As I bent in jagged pursuit, my schoolmates ran away, shrieking with fear and delight, so involved that they failed to notice the schoolhouse door opening. From the eye of the hurricane, *as* the eye of the hurricane, I noticed, unable to do a damn thing about it. The bicycle seemed to have a mind of its own as it held a course directly for Reb Tellman.

He stood in the doorway until the last possible moment. At the precise instant he leapt aside, I yanked the wheel sharply and came to the same elegant sideways halt as the previous owner. So that was how to do it, I thought; but crashing would have been wiser.

Reb Tellman poked his head cautiously back into the frame, then rose to his full height, sputtering with indignation. "What is this, a circus? In. In!"

Nobody else said a word, least of all Moshele Rosen, who looked at me as if I had walked into the classroom stark naked. Throughout the day, one after another of my classmates would turn in their seats to gaze at me with shock, wonder, and a newfound respect. I think they thought that I had murdered the murderous gypsy child in order to steal his bicycle. My scrawny arms and thin, side-curled profile assumed heroic stature. I was the shape of revelation. After school, I pedaled lightly, granting a backward nod and a cavalier wave to those who had thought they knew me, and now knew better.

At home, however, they were not impressed. My father watched me careen within inches of his vest button with the same mild curiosity he might have accorded the thrashings of a half-dead flounder.

My mother said, "Your quilt's not upstairs."

They had not discussed this, and my father stroked his chin as he digested the information. It didn't take him long. "How did you get the bicycle?" he asked.

I gulped. "I traded them."

"You what?" burst forth from both simultaneously.

This gave me strength. If they had expected the answer, it should not have surprised them. If, then, the surprise was mock, so was the outrage. I repeated myself with the utmost dignity.

They looked at me as if I were Esau caught trading his birthright for a bowl of pottage. It was an accurate comparison. True, the deal may have been stupid, a point which I heatedly denied. "Yes, I will miss my quilt," I said. "But the question is whether it was mine to choose to miss."

"Of course it's yours, but. . . . "

"But what? But only as far as the doorway? But only as far as the front gate? There are no 'buts.'"

"Maybe," they said. Maybe! I was ecstatic. My parents were kind, but they were firm. "Maybe" was nothing short of miraculous. Maybe it was the power of my bicycle that had won them over as it had won over my classmates, as it had triumphed over Reb Tellman. What a vehicle!

For a few days I was happy. Proszowice was a maze I had mastered, and the bicycle took me through its labyrinth as swiftly as my fingers had once crossed from menorah to bunny to train. I cornered the synagogue in the shade of the eaves, nicked a doorknob off the tavern, and breezed down the center of Kastel Street into the square, where I circled old Otto IV until his head nearly spun on its marble neck. I did figure eights around the baffled horses, laughing at the farmers. I rode with one hand, rode with no hands, closed my eyes and pedaled on pure instinct. When my brother urged me to hurry, I said: "No sweat. You go on ahead. I'll catch up." Sure enough, by the time his toes were numb, I had swept around the final corner, alit, and opened the door with seconds to spare. Reb Tellman glared suspiciously from the window of the cheder.

Everyone at school, except for Reb Tellman and Moshele, begged for a chance to try my bicycle. "Sure, " I said, certain that no one could stay upright. They slipped back, pitched forward, or simply toppled over like drunken soldiers. If it was prominence I had gained by "stealing" the bicycle, in subduing it I had earned prestige. Notwithstanding the trouble I had that first morning, I really did take to cycling, and soon felt incomplete without my wheels. I might have had them for legs and handlebars for arms and the gears for guts, for the road was my natural element. Intoxicated by speed and mobility, I was glad to overlook a poor night's sleep.

My bed was a raft adrift at sea. I curled up to avoid the blustery chill, but it penetrated my new woolen blanket like cheese-cloth. Shipwrecked, buffeted mercilessly by the winds and swells, I was subject to any random peril of the deep. A slimy octopus tentacle crept toward me like a giant finger. When it touched my lips, I woke, hastily quitting the briny abyss for the only safe mooring I had—you guessed it, my bike.

This harbor was doubly secure because my sole rival for berth never returned. A small gypsy girl came in his stead. She had the same dark eyes and dark hair in a braid that hung down to the small of her back. She wore an old fortune-teller's gown embroidered with mysterious astrological symbols and had a tear that exposed a narrow triangle of golden calf. We assumed that she was his sister, although she was nothing at all like my little sister—or anything my little sister would ever become.

Like her brother, the gypsy girl had the mark of perpetual cold upon her. The faint blue tinge of her upper lip gave this away, but in her case it was not the result of the weather outside but the climate within. Her cold would freeze a quilt. She hated us. You could see it in her stance: legs spread, arms locked akimbo, she dared us to buy or not to buy her wares, a statue of defiance that made Otto IV look like a candle softening in the sun. She

would not haggle, would not fawn, would simply wait until someone lay down the money or bartered goods for a mere gypsy locket.
Yet with her hostile pose she drew a stream of customers, as if
the Proszowicer were afraid to let her go a day without a sale,
afraid she would stay the night, legs spread, arms akimbo, frozen
solid by her own frigid spleen by morning. At dusk she would
load up her bag with turnips and onions and her tribe's daily bread.
Lacking a bicycle to transport them, she hoisted the foodstuffs onto
her frail back.

I could feel the bag's cord cut into my own shoulder.

I recalled my father's words about the repercussions of fish. I
thought of the harm I had done to this young girl with her heavy
burden and sped to make amends. "Excuse me, " I said. "May I
help you?"

Her eyes flashed recognition. "I would rather have my legs
cut off!"

I rode aimlessly about the open square in wide, contemplative
arcs and stopped short of collisions with a mental jolt. Since I had
given up sleep the bicycle had become my comfort, but the sharp
words of the gypsy girl slashed its tires. Why? Here I had made
an honest trade, had, in fact, offered to remedy any inequity. And
what response had I received? I was treated as the creature I had
heard called "Jew."

I saw a potato lying at the edge of the market. It must have
dropped through a hole in her bag. I scooped it off the ground
like an eagle pouncing on a field mouse. In the process, I glimpsed
another potato some twenty meters down the road. I picked that
one up too, and then another. The earth-encrusted lumps eased me
oddly. Cradled against my belly with one hand while the other
steered and dove for more, they were a nourishing solace.

The people of Proszowice were good, godfearing folk, but
slow. They were potatoes when I craved red peppers. Look at me,
zipping past the graybeards weighed down by their Bibles. Unbent
by circumstance, I was taller, quicker than the villagers. I was of
a new, frictionless generation to whom the old laws did not apply.

I was a perpetual-motion machine. I did not need sleep. I was a gypsy. Bearing potatoes, I would join my kind to see the world. They would remark my bond to their bicycle and welcome me. The young girl would not want her legs amputated.

I was led southward, gathering potatoes. Following the path, I pedaled swiftly past the town cemetery, where I heard the whistling of the spirits lodged there and saw a few stray feathers dancing in the wind. I kept pumping until I lost sight of the wrought-iron fence. I began to pedal faster and faster, rolling up and down hills as if they were no higher than the mounds of my erstwhile quilt. Lulled by the regular click of the wheels, I continued into the thick of the forest that eventually lead into the Carpathian Mountains. The sweat of my exertion staved off the cold. Then suddenly the potatoes stopped. Perhaps she had adjusted the position of the bag. Perhaps the rent had sealed itself.

The trees loomed with deep green singleness, and I felt that I had passed through a curtain into another world. The leaves were a million eyes watching me, and the branches plucked at my yarmulke. Even the light was qualitatively different here. In addition to the distant lamp of the moon, the earth seemed to glow. It was the indirect illumination of a campfire burning in a shallow ravine by the side of the road.

A slope was cut into the wall of the ravine, but it was still treacherous. The bicycle slid on the loose dirt and threatened to plummet. At an especially sharp curve I was able to see the fire and hear its music. A flute and a violin wove in sinuous harmony through the warp of the flames, which became more vivid as I descended. It was a lively tune that might have been cheerful had it been played on any instrument other than the mournful strings, and it broke off when I entered the circle of light. The murmur of conversation was noticeable by its absence.

A strong, middle-aged woman was stirring the brew in a large black kettle on a tripod over the fire. About five dark youths sat ranged in a crescent around a heavyset, middle-aged chieftain whose features looked familiar. Horses were tethered to a nearby trailer.

One figure sat apart from the others. He was on the opposite side of the fire, wrapped in my quilt like an old lady.

They all stared at me.

"Music!" a voice, music itself, the bells to match the missing violin, came from the trailer. It was the gypsy girl. She was stroking her unbraided hair with a mother-of-pearl brush destined to finance the next day's dinner. It was a silvery barrel carried over a jet waterfall. She parted the waves. "Why is there no mus..." she halted.

"Here," I said. You dropped these," and the potatoes fell from my lap and rolled until they stopped and stood like rocks. Without them, I felt unarmed, afraid, and very, very cold. The momentum of the bicycle still throbbed in my chest and legs and groin. Once more I had been drawn to the brink by my enthusiasm, but I was so physically and emotionally drained that I could not distinguish between the danger and my own most trivial desire. I was simultaneously ecstatic and abject. Above all, I was cold, so cold I threw caution to the winds, laid the bicycle down, and stepped to the campfire to warm my hands.

The violin recommenced a low melody.

One of the young men was holding a club. He threw it idly into the air and caught it with ominous ease. He did this the way Isaac the Millionaire flipped a gold ruble, but the next time I looked at him there were two clubs tossing. From the darkness, a third club emerged, and a fourth joined the pack. One after another, they fell and floated back up in dreamy suspension, as if repelled by the twitching wrist of the dark-skinned lad. His poise and dexterity were so great that I felt like applauding. Without missing a beat, he dipped each club into a can of liquid that turned to flame when touched to the embers. He juggled the blazing clubs over his head, under his knees, behind his back, in sparkling pinwheels.

The heavyset man watched the spectacle, nodding with approval. When his son had more or less subsided, he slapped his coarse palms on his thighs and squatted, whereupon a second youth leapt onto his back, locked ankles around his father's neck, and slapped his thighs in turn. A child no more than seven years old sprang on top of him. Now the father straightened, twelve feet tall with his filial burden, a triple-torsoed, three-headed monster.

It was the girl's turn. Scowling and flipping her glorious mane, she strode to the tree. When she turned, she had a rose clenched between her ivory teeth. Her baby brother, atop the gypsy totem pole, revealed a knife like the knife Moshele had bought and flung it through the circle of blazing clubs. It severed the bud from the stem, not an inch from his sister's lips.

Only the boy who had traded me the bicycle and his mother remained passive. Their grim taciturnity was as intimidating as the skill of the performers.

The violin faded to a whisper, the clubs were doused, the small boy jumped from the youth's shoulders, the youth alit from the man. Leaving the knife behind, the girl strung a rope from the tree to a hook at the top of the trailer. I hadn't noticed, but a ladder was leaning against the trailer. It was waiting.

I looked to the boy in the quilt for an answer to my unspoken question. Yes, I had initiated the confrontation, so it was only fair that the gypsies choose the weapons. But what were the stakes? Was it to be a bowl of soup or black-magic pagan rituals? The boy was mute, yet the chill shrug of his shoulders under the padding of the quilt was reassuring. The menorahs and bunnies and trains winked in the flickering light. The same vague sense of necessity that had compelled me to follow the gypsy girl to their fire now drove me up the rungs. I knew neither what I expected nor what was expected of me, but I felt confident until I reached the top. The bicycle was there.

I inched one foot tentatively onto the rope and extended my arms. I dragged the rear foot forward. Tilting first to the left, then overcompensating to the right, I stood. Otto IV I wasn't, but I was upright. I stepped back, straddled the bicycle, and rolled the front wheel out. The rope sagged, then went taut. I lifted my feet to the pedals, closed my eyes, and pushed off. I opened my eyes. The gypsies were six feet below me, but it might as well have been miles. I felt their eyes concentrating on me as on a distant star that would disappear with any random blink. Time stood still in the presence of perfect motion.

At the tree, I bent carefully to pluck the rosebud out from under the knife. Halfway back to the trailer, I threw the flower to the girl—who threw it into the fire.

I fell, and the arms of the strong man caught me.

The bicycle lay mangled. The boy to whom it rightfully belonged cried out in pain. He jumped up from under my quilt to kneel by the side of the twisted machine, soothing it as he would a wounded beast.

For the first time, the gypsy girl looked at me with sadness rather than hatred. I think she smiled.

"Go home," she said. "You've earned it."

I did not understand. I thought that the prizes I had ridden the high wire for were the bicycle, the girl—the whole wide world. How could I reemigrate to the home I had spurned? "Wait," I wanted to cry. "You've got me all wrong. I'm not afraid. I belong here."

But the girl and her father were already taking down the long rope. They were coiling it from both ends, the twin circles like the wheels of the bicycle, which the brothers were busy rewiring. The mother was peeling potatoes. Immersed in their domestic routine, they no longer had time for a wandering Jew.

Standing alone, I thought I saw the remains of my quilt aglow in the gypsy hearth. Actually it was the quilt itself I saw through the fire. Colored by the flame but unconsumed, it spoke to me. Every square told its story, each the same story—my story. (The hero aspires to a land that offers him both beauty and jeopardy; it is his bed. He is wise to embark in the finest ship, his quilt.) That was the prize I had sought, and found.

Wrapped in my legacy, I walked home.

Sincerely,

Yours

saac the Millionaire was in love. "I have met a lady," he said, "of the first degree."

The chorus of afternoon prayer ground to a discontinuous mutter. There was turbulence, then an anxious calm. A bench scraped, a book fell, and old man Medisky jumped to bring it to his lips in atonement.

"A lady of such many and varied accomplishments. A lady of such rare and exquisite charm. A lady of such property."

With each word we fought the harder to lean back, but not a voice was rasied against Isaac, nor an ear turned from him.

"A lady of such breeding and beauty—"

"Yes," the Doctor whispered.

"—as to boggle the mind," Isaac concluded, and rocked back on his heels in mute appreciation, radiating joy, as he did when money was present.

And the spell was broken. "How dare you!" the Rabbi thundered, and the congregation echoed their outraged accord. They turned as one to cast out the intruder.

"But no, you do not understand," Isaac pleaded. "I make the announcement of my plight here, because if God, blessed be He, is good enough to give me this paragon of all possible virtues, I shall endow the synagogue with a new ark of marble, silver, and gold."

There was a hesitant lull. We had misjudged Isaac.

"And a curtain of the finest silk, embroidered with purple and indigo thread."

Isaac was forgiven. Still, he was told that although his intentions were admirable, his choice of a platform from which to announce them was not.

"Alas, but I know that!" he wailed. "But I cannot suppress my feelings. Neither have I the capacity to properly reveal them. I am at a loss," and he and the rest of us turned a sorrowful eye toward the splintery wooden box and tattered curtains Isaac had promised to replace with a truly fitting repository for the word of the Holy One, blessed be He. "I came because, well yes, first because I cannot contain myself, and second to beg of you all, and especially You" (his eyes raised), "help in attaining my deepest desire, a lady. Yes, a lady of such magnificence . . . "

"Enough, Isaac." It was the Rabbi, kind when need be. "But this is not the place. We shall give it thought and pray for an answer to your problems."

"Thank you. Thank you so much. From the bottom of my heart . . . "

Enough, Isaac!"

"Yes, certainly," he said, and repeated as he backed out from the sanctuary and went back to business.

Aside from his frequent outbursts of passion, Isaac did not live any differently than anyone else, even though he was a millionaire. Of course he kept two horses to our one, and a suite of rooms at Proszowice's only hotel, and a radio; but he still prayed at the same disrepaired shul we did, and he wore the same shiny gabardines we did, and he ate the same herring. Well, almost the same herring. But Isaac was a millionaire. How we knew this I couldn't say, unless it was Isaac himself who told us; but that it was a fact we were certain. We knew it like we knew the sun to rise in the east.

Once Isaac was questioned as to his financial standing by Pleskin, his landlord. The object of doubt drew himself up to every inch of his five feet and three inches, bursting with barely contained apopleptic fury. Enunciating every syllable, he said, "Are you insinuating" (repeating so that everyone could hear), "I say, are you daring to insinuate that I do not have the pittance owed you" (as if he were not the one who did the owing), "that my credit is not good here?"

"I did not say that. But neither have I seen the rent for six months."

"You want to see the rent. You really want to see the rent, you, you, you . . . pipsqueak!" Isaac stormed from the room, leaving us to think that maybe that was the last of him; for although there was no doubt that he was a millionaire, none of us had seen his money either. Grumbling in the lobby increased in proportion to the minutes passed, after ten too many of which Isaac returned. His choler having subsided, he was smug as a bug as he drew a carefully stacked and banded pile of banknotes from his grubby gray jacket's right-hand pocket. There was a ten-zloty bill on one side and a ten-zloty bill on the other and at least a hundred more in between. From his left pocket Isaac reaped another similarly packed sheaf. His vest yielded one final fortune. "Now," he said into the dumbfounded silence, "How much do I owe you? We shall settle accounts and I shall find lodging elsewhere."

"Isaac. Isaac. Calm down," Pleskin said. "Your credit is ace. I don't know what came over me. Take that back to your rooms. Please, don't offend me."

"I insist," Isaac the Millionaire demanded.

"*I* insist," the innkeeper remonstrated.

"In that case . . ." Isaac tarried, clearly relishing the suspense, "I accept."

Never mind that Isaac later confided to me that between one of the banknotes and the other was newspaper. He was, and to me ever will be, Isaac the Millionaire. Why, we were proud to be owed money by such a man.

Isaac was nearly seventy years old, but beneath his beard, as gray and venerable as any wise man's, lay the hairless ardor of an adolescent. He was consumed by the twin passions of the innocent: money and love. According to his record, self-recorded, the former generally sufficed, but when it failed the latter was always there to soothe the hurt. Isaac fell in love as regularly as moonrise. On beholding *her,* his eyes narrowed with thought, widened with beatific vision, then set in stupified rapture.

During the weeks in which the passion of Isaac was ascendant all Proszowice was in thrall. From my father's store to the market to the barber to the back rows of the one-room schoolhouse there were discussions of whether he would succeed and whether he should, whether his would-be conquests were deserving of him—for not all were the paragons he thought them. Some were rich and some were beautiful, but one limped and another was mean. Until the lady from Cracow, whose discovery provoked his grand offer to the synagogue, it was love itself rather than the beloved that held him in sway. Perpetually pierced by Cupid's pointed arrows, he willingly succumbed, and from the contagion of his romantic delirium, so did we. And when success was his, as it invariably was, we all rejoiced. The marriage feasts were renowned for kilometers around, and the lucky lady or her father was glad to pay.

Unfortunately, Isaac's passion always outlasted his women. Oh, they married him all right, but then they died. Grippes, agues, and catarrhs spirited them away almost as fast as he could find them. They fell down stairs and through holes in the ice. One (why, he could never fathom) took poison. Another was struck by lightning. And one, the blind one, wandered into the forest and died of starvation. But this did not stop them from coming, one and all, young and old, virgins and widows (for Isaac was catholic in his tastes), to taste the wonders of this wonderful man. Still they continued to surrender to the curious fortune they could not best, and as Isaac had yearned for them, so he beat his breast and mourned for them the requisite eleven months—after which he found another, only to mourn her as well.

What did I have to do with these events? By now I should think that would be obvious. I, at the tender age of twelve, not yet a man, was Isaac's procurer. As surely as any pagan emperor's emissary sent to the slave market with a purse full of gold, or a Moscow madame introducing a gentleman to her girls, I brought Isaac and his women together by means of my words. You see, in order to serve his amours, Isaac made me into a writer. I never found out how he knew that just such a talent was mine to cultivate. One may as well ask how he knew which women had the seed within them that would respond to his nourishment; but that he chose me with the same care with which he chose his many doomed wives was apparent.

It all started with my father's herring. Good herring it was, from the Baltic Sea, tender and lightly salted, sold whole or deboned, but, frankly, not any different from that sold by the other two grocers in Proszowice. Of course, my father raved about his herring, but so did the other grocers. For us, however, it was a natural step from the sign on the barrel that read "Herring" to "Finest Herring," and from there to "Savory as the sweetmeats of King Solomon's time," and on to large placards chronicling the journey of the fish from "the depths of the Scandinavian Sea" to the nets of the fishermen and "overland through blackest night" to reach Proszowice in time for the breakfast table of Mrs. Horowitz and her three unmarried daughters. "Sealed and certified by the Herring Master of Petersburg Harbor as of the first degree" my father's herring was, and "Unconditionally guaranteed to tickle the most fickle of taste buds." You will, I hope, be able to guess the author.

Isaac the Millionaire always claimed that it was "that little liar of a son you have" that made him owe us, rather than Kleiner or Bobover, money. Actually, it was the softness of my father's heart and his reluctance to claim debts from a man who was almost always in mourning that convinced Isaac to drive his two horses up to our door and ask for "a bit of the finest, freshest herring to be found between Minsk and Paris," as if he were buying it only because I, so small and insignificant in the corner, had coerced him.

He was a splendid man, Isaac the Millionaire was, joyful and generous to a fault. If only he hadn't cheated and stolen and persisted in losing what he cheated and stole to sharpies more skillful than himself. But what did it matter? "We'll never have the money he hasn't got," my father would say, ungrammatical, ambiguous, acute. "But neither will we starve."

Between the two of them, Isaac detailing his latest foreign coup and my father bemoaning his wholesaler's price increase on the "smelly scavengers," they nibbled half of the herring right there. This gave rise to a philosophical question: Did Isaac eat my father's herring by not paying for what he ate, or did my father eat the herring that he had sold to Isaac? The greasy stack of wax paper piled up as they smacked their lips, laughed and cried with each other.

"Such a scamp you have there!" Isaac would say.

My father would smile.

And I would modestly bow my head with the weight of the pleasure I felt.

Perhaps Isaac had seen *Cyrano* at the State Theater. If so, he should have cast me as a rival. I supposed that he knew I did not approve of that year's particular match, a local seamstress with a bit too much heft about her stern (she of the thin ice on the first day of spring). In any case, Isaac made the offer that was to transform me from Proszowice's second greatest liar into a writer. Two years and two wives ago, he had given me a chocolate and asked, "So scamp, do you think you could tailor your literary talents to anything besides herring?"

I lifted my head with the first stirrings of pride and desire. I knew exactly what he meant.

Now Isaac was hardly a nonverbal man himself and could have had his own winged words transcribed, but there was something so foreign to him yet native to me in the act of writing that it seemed appropriate that I write for him. Of course, I did not yet understand the feelings he laid claim to, but, after all, what did I know about herring?

We sat aside, huddled in the corner of my father's store, isolated from the customers whom it was my after-school duty to serve, while Isaac explained the passions to me. They seemed very strange—"a weight on the heart" one sentence, "the heart like a bird" the next—until I realized that it was just that essence of contradiction that made them what they were. It was a matter of opposing forces, ecstasy and anxiety, that both produced and subsequently tore at the unique personality of Isaac the Millionaire. The heart like a weighty bird? "My soul to thee flies upward," I translated in the heroic mode.

"Yes," Isaac beamed. "You have it ... just like Shakespeare." And when I asked the inevitable, he explained, "An Englishman." And sighed, "We will have to do something about that."

Inspired by Isaac's expanded explanation, I rephrased Prince Hamlet's famous lines to his beloved Lady Macbeth:

> To be or not to be
> With you is the question.
> Whether tis nobler in the heart
> To endure the slings and arrows
> Of tremendous passion
> Or by taking you into my arms
> End them.

Isasc's confidence had not been misplaced. Before I could malappropriate my way through his versions of *Lear* and *Othello,* the seamstress was caught in my web of words and Isaac was smiling at me from beneath the bridal canopy. But the ice was already melting.

During Isaac's next courtship, I extended the boundaries of my literary territory by toying with a sacrilege he would never commit. In his name, I told the baker's twenty-five-year-old maiden daughter (better she had remained that way: fever) that when I saw her "across the barrier which separates our sexes, the unholy wakes in me, and the Rabbi's warnings of temptation speak to me. Let us make legal this before it devours us ... "

Whether the Rabbi had actually spoken of temptation made no difference, for all the girl could remember was the lewdly enticing smile of the man in the gray vest and gold (-plated) watchchain and the way he twirled the hairs of his beard. Whether Hamlet took Lady Macbeth in his arms made no difference either. It was Isaac himself rather than my letters on his behalf that won over the female heart. Bearing a purity of love it had never before encountered, the weaker of the species could not but yield.

Similarly, women resigned themselves to the strange curse that haunted the objects of Isaac's love. Each thought she would prove the exception, but somewhere in the sepia tints of the wedding daguerrotype was the foreshadowning of doom. Since each new tragedy would lead to another collaboration between its author and myself, I was not altogether unhappy about this state of affairs. Reprehensible, yes, but our letters were the only literary exercise I got aside from herring, pickles, and, occasionally, cheese. I wished them no ill, but I needed the loss of the wives as much as Isaac needed the wives. And if such were the will of the Holy One, blessed be He, who were we to question it? There was such a sad inevitability to the women's untimely ends that a mournful humor was born of their demise.

"Poor woman!" people would say when Isaac turned amorous.

"Zalman the Digger will have food for the Shabbos," they said.

"Isaac," my father said one when he thought I wasn't back from school yet. "I don't think your romances wrong, but I wonder for my son. He is a child. Is it good, I mean this . . . writing? He thinks of nothing but the words to fit your . . . exuberance."

"Hush, my friend. Do we remember David as the king of Israel? No, he is the psalm singer. You have another Sholom Aleichem here. A Mendele Mocher. Maybe a Bialik." And visions of the great Hebrew poet danced before my father's eyes. He was a good man and pious, but no more so than his neighbors. He realized that there were as many pathways to God as there were men to follow them. Perhaps those who wrote the prayers were more likely than those who recited them to attain the heavenly realm. Also, he saw that something had been lit in me, as in my mentor, and that flame he would not deny me. For Hanukkah that year, he bought me a book of poetry and inscribed it, "To my son, who writes his own, the words of others, from his father." I treasured that book.

As usual after a bereavement, Isaac obeyed the ritual week of mourning and the ten months and three weeks of continence. Of the pleasures dear to him only business was exempt from the strictures of the law, and so during the latter ten-plus months he threw himself into a scheme to reestablish the monarchist government of Czechoslovakia. In itself this would hardly have appealed to Isaac's egalitarian nature, but he happened to hold the keys to a barnful of antique korunas that his puppet prince was to declare coin of the realm on coronation day—which, needless to say, never came. By the time it was impossible to assert that it ever would, however, the year had passed and Isaac was able to turn once again to his true love, Love.

He exhibited his characteristic preoccupation, his idiot's manner; but this time something was different. There was the scene in the synagogue and the offer of a reward, as if in his desperation Isaac were attempting to bribe the Holy One, blessed be He. Then, when Romeo approached me as a prelude to our usual collaboration, he mentioned not only his new Juliet, but the others, whom he had previously let lie in blissful repose. "My little conspirator, Scamp," he said so sadly that I knew the days of my scamphood were over, "she is the real thing, blessed be the souls of my dearly departed past wives, but a man must live. The heart knows no bounds."

Isaac was so beclouded that he wanted to take me to Cracow, but my father thought this was dangerous. When Isaac claimed that he needed me to research the recipient of the letters I was to write, my father pointed out that research had never been necessary before. Deftly outflanking these logical qualms, Isaac attacked my father's soft spot, asking, "How can you deny the boy?" and the battle was almost won. My father fell back on poverty, but Isaac whisked this last defense out from under him by offering to pay. My father in turn objected, but the millionaire would have none of that. "Nonsense!" he said. "I'd be happy to. I owe you enough money already, so if you insist on being foolish you can take it off my tab." From this unprecedented bid my father realized the true depth of Isaac's desire and, from an imploring puppy expression, mine. Between the old man and the young boy he was lost. He made me promise to keep up with my studies during the week we would be gone.

I leapt to hug my father and Isaac threw his own short arms around the two of us. There, by the barrels of herring, whole and deboned, that had started it all, we three embraced.

The great boulevard stretched as far as the steppes, and every inch of it was packed like a kaleidoscope. The sheer din of daily life, the trams, the horses, the voices of the newsboys crying their tidings, was a cacophonous delight. Smells of such pungent variety assaulted me that I nearly went mad with desire until Isaac told me they weren't kosher.

I felt the metropolis throbbing in my veins. It was too big, too diverse, too difficult to grasp, until Issac brought me to the purest distillation of urbanity. This was a giant gingerbread cake of marble, metal, and glass with gilt frosting. Two sculpted women held aloft globes of light on either side of the twin brass doors, from between which poured forth the light of the interior, a glimpse of heaven through its gates, ebony moldings framing ivory walls, and a crimson carpet leading to another door, the holy of holies, the amphitheater.

Milling about, emerging from one noble carriage after another and announced by costumed footmen, were people such as I had never seen before, people to vie with the angels, whose abode their abodes vied with. The men were tall and slim, and some of them wore medals and others had moustaches as pointed as the hand of a compass. But the women were the true glory of the place, and I could see the lure that had captured my friend. They were as perfect as dolls, with wide eyes, bee-stung lips, and translucent skin, and their fragrance was headier than a barrelful of the Baltic's finest scavengers.

Isaac looked down at me, smiled, took my hand in one of his, and with the other gestured to the scene before us. In a rare moment of simplicity, he said, "My child . . . the opera."

It was as much to effect this reverence in me as to show me the woman of his dreams and my prose that Isaac the Millionaire took me to the opera. Of course, this would subsequently enhance my writing. Now that I knew there was more to this world than herring, I wanted my words to sing like those of the sainted Puccini.

Isaac nudged me during intermission. "There . . . there she is," he sighed; and there, indeed, she was. Her clothes were of the same jeweled quality as her elder companion's and there was something of the same angular grace about her features. Wobbling on her first set of heels, just as I itched in my first pair of long pants, she was as keenly aware of the seduction inherent in her thin legs as I was of the manly strength beneath my wool.

"Mark your target well," Isaac whispered to me.

"I have," I said. Yes, I was as smitten by the girl as Isaac was by the woman.

The Théâtre d'Opéra everpresent in my mind, my father's store and the one-room school seemed beneath contempt. Nor did the other children believe my tales of operatic splendor. Heathens, they laughed, "Go back to your herring!" and asked, "Are you sure you didn't swim to the depths of the Scandinavian Sea?" Never able to speak with the fluency I commanded on paper, in my indignation I grew even more inarticulate. I turned red with impotent fury and retreated in a huff to my memory and my books and my love letters.

"Words cannot express . . . " I began, knowing full well how false that statement prefacing my expression in words was but struck enough by my predicament to believe it.

"Words cannot express," I began, "what I feel. How pitiful the pen in the face of a desire greater than Caesar's for empire. How small my voice when seven strong tenors could not do you justice. How weak any human voice before the sensibility that spurs it forward, as mine now races before me, to reveal to you all that it endures in the name of love.

"LOVE. . . .

"But my thoughts outrun me. And perhaps I shock you. I admit that we have not been formally introduced. I admit that I only know thee from afar, but would fain close the distance I have already o'erleaped in my heart. . . . "

I went on to the specific—her lips, her eyes, and to the universal—the celestial. I outshone myself for my friend, but I was also working for myself, deliberately inserting passages with double meanings. By calling the passion of the aged "new," I meant naive. I mentioned its birth rather than its fruition, and I did not use comparisons, for, unlike Isaac, I had no basis on which to make them. For I was addressing not one but two ladies.

Somewhere inside a boudoir like a cave, its draped and pleated purple curtains guarding against the sun, its crystal and porcelain surfaces dank with mysterious feminine odors, she wandered. Inquisitive as a baby goose, she ran her tiny hands over the flasks and vials and atomizers, and poked into drawers and closets, and crawled under the enormous canopied bed, from which she peered through the hanging folds of silken coverlet. She daubed scent behind her ears and weighed herself down with golden booty, and in the dim light of a laquered Chinese lantern she read the letters her elder received and giggled—until she read mine. It was smothered in the smell of the elder, having been pressed to the heart touched so often by fingers that in turn touched the lips of the aromatic dispensers, and was shredding from constant folding and unfolding, reading and rereading; but within it was something still virgin, a sentiment waiting for one who could comprehend it. She silently gathered to herself the folds of the gown she was wearing and curled up in the corner of the canopied bed, her head on the square, down-filled pillow, to ponder her unknown admirer.

The power of words—I professed it; I believed it. Still, somewhere, maybe nearby the mysterious wellspring of emotion harkened to in my letters, I was surprised. Miracle of miracles, the lady's pink envelope appeared!

Her reply was civil, but the fact that she had replied at all proved that a volcano lay beneath the calm. Isaac and I poured over every word and imagained inflection. "I have received your kind letter," she began as if it were an invitation to a flower show, "and read it with most eager interest."

"*Most* eager," Isaac whooped.

"Seldom does a lady receive such declarations and still more seldom is she in a position to acknowledge them. Most coincidentally, though, I will be on a tour of some of my properties later this autumn and look forward to the meeting you suggest."

Isaac nearly swooned.

Between one communication and the next, the days of summer flew by like birds. Isaac devoured schools of herring in the corner of my father's store while he and I plotted the furtherance of his romantic strategy, and I plotted the furtherance of my own. As the exchanges became conversational as well as rhetorical, I introduced myself—just one of the many local characters. In the midst of enticements to the lady (Proszowice's opera house) I dropped hints to the girl (the culture of the young people).

But my words could not pave streets, and what would my father's shop look like beside the department store the ladies had inherited (it took up an entire blockfront on Szolny Square)? Could the ragamuffin poet Isaac the Millionaire had taken under his wing live up to the swells of the opera?

I began to hedge against the facts, to write that "the roads of this world, whether marble or dirt, are as nothing to the roads to my heart, which pounds, day and night, for you." "And of that heart," I also wrote, "what building could I erect to replace its mansion, each chamber dedicated solely to you . . . " I used every epistolary means at my command to mitigate the awful truth, but sometimes I felt plain hopeless.

Isaac the Millionaire laughed. "Look here," he riffled the stack of delicate pink correspondence. "Signposts on the highway of love." He rubbed his hands together and leaned back. "We shall have her," he said. "It was meant to be."

I was not reassured by Isaac's blithe repetition of my roads-to-the-heart theory. Those were words for a willing victim, words I had crafted to manipulate and distort; I would not be fooled by my own trickery.

Yes, they were coming. The date was set. Proszowice was the same filthy town it had always been. Along with the Proszowicer peeking from behind closed shutters, I thought that there would be dire consequences to the visit. It was axiomatic that rank entailed ruin, and if the prelates and generals who had laid us waste had at least not been misled, who knew what catastrophe this episode of the two big mouths was leading to? But Isaac the Millionaire calmly signed the tab for another herring and sat picking his teeth. "Nonsense!" he declared to my and everyone else's objections. "The new ark is as good as installed. Smile, Rabbi!"

My father looked at me with benign, baffled curiosity. He thought he was witnessing the nervousness of the playwright on opening night rather than that of an actor in the drama. If only he knew what lay between the lines! Even Isaac was not aware that we were more than allies: we were brothers.

I didn't even know if *she* was coming.

Isaac recounted the time when he was smuggling diamonds into Prague in a shipment of soap powder and the barge went down in one of the city's twisted canals. The bubbles caused havoc, but by morning the statues of the kings had never been cleaner. "Still have the medal to prove my service to the empire. Never did recover the gems. A small price to pay, eh? . . . do you hear something?" His ears perked up. "They'll be here any minute."

"They?"

"The lady and her entourage."

There was no time for explanations, but I was sure he knew my secret, that old man. We smoothed our clothes and set our faces in a welcome demeanor and turned to each other for approval. My God, blessed be Thou, what could we have seen?—an aged Lothario pretending he was half his age and a wishful-thinking child pretending he was twice his. To each other we looked great.

The four jet horses simultaneously reared in impressive display. I saw a red and black coat of arms, wolves on a field, rampant. A phalanx of servants clustered beside the door, from which a white-gloved hand fluttered for Isaac to help his lady alight into the mud. When asked later how she knew instantly, exactly, who he was, she answered, "I was on the road to his heart. How could I have missed my destination?" She was as poetic as he was.

"And this must be the young writer," she added with a smile that was more than merely polite; it was knowing. What sort of ghost was I that everyone could see? So what! Did Isaac not inspire and endorse everything that was said in my letters? Was it not the inner feelings that mattered, and were they not true? But the lady knew this. She would not have come to Proszowice otherwise. Given this knowledge, nothing could have kept her away. She did not mind living in Pleskin's hotel or paying the bill for it. She was at home on our country avenues as long as her arm was enwrapped in Isaac's. She had as generous a capacity and as tremendous a need for happiness as he. Their marriage would last forever. "And this," she said, "is my grand-daughter."

She was a spoiled angel who insisted on the luxury her grandmother willingly did without. Of course, the haughty servants from her big-city home were glad to provide this, and of course so was I. Thus I thought that I would earn the serenity of the elderly couple whose romance held the whole town in its spell.

"This place disgusts me," my darling sneered, and I promised to take her away. "Where?" she pouted, and I told her of the shores of the Scandinavian Sea. "How?" she demanded, so I borrowed two ten-zloty notes from my friend and cut up a stack of newspapers. "Big deal."

The new ark shone like the skin of the lady standing before it, its opalescent marble veined as hers with barely visible streaks of red and blue, its face glowing as hers. Even its dress was as splendid as hers for this special occasion, midnight blue, with threads of gold and silver spelling out "From Isaac. For Blessings Received." Once again, Isaac smiled at me as he broke the wineglass with the heel of his boot.

The shabby finery of Proszowice mixed uneasily with Cracow's smart set at the reception. All of the good women surrounded the bride while the men conferred with the groom, but the final link between society and shtetl was forged when the lady tilted back her perfect head and, pinching the morsel above it with her perfectly shaped fingers, opened her perfect mouth and dropped into it a nearly perfect herring. "Their descriptions are matched only by their taste," she said, once again smiling at their author.

My love? She left. Her mother was horrified at her grandmother's inauspicious marriage and took the opportunity to steal away the flower girl. We corresponded, of course, but the frequency with which we did so diminished. My letters under my own name were pallid and uninspired compared to their anonymous ancestors. I hated to admit it, but as Isaac until he met his lady, as she before him, I was in love with the idea of love. And letters. And so, not too long after the memory of my first correspondent had begun to fade, I finally abandoned all pretense of writing to her and invented imaginary girls to write to, and imaginary romances.

Of course, I liked it and ate it (for a good many years I practically lived on it), but I never really took to my father's herring as much as I said I did.

The Woman

with a

Dog

hivka Bellet was a shrew. Her voice, her look, her manner were a gall she imposed like a tax on anyone who came close to her, and the closer they were, the harsher she was. Her friends, neighbors, relatives, the workers she employed, and the shopkeepers she patronized all felt the bitter sting of her companionship; but first among the victims was her husband, Hirsh David.

Morning to night Shivka nagged, scolded, insulted him, and no matter where he was or what he was doing, our one local tycoon was at the virago's beck and call. Fancy clothes and chocolates were hers for the griping, and one day, "An organ, you uncultured boor!" She had been lolling in bed, flipping the pages of a fashionable review when she came across it and said, "If the Countess Rogazcy has an organ, you would deprive your wife? Is she any better than I?"

"No, my dear. No, my pet. Of course she isn't. I will be in Cracow next week and I will look for one."

"Next week! I should wait seven days. God created the world in six and you can't get me a lousy organ."

"Tomorrow, my mouse. Tomorrow I will go to Cracow."

"Tomorrow? I could die in my sleep, and I should never have had an organ like the Countess Rogazcy whom you think is better than I am."

"I am on my way." And not once did Hirsh David realize how outrageous the demands of his beloved were. He was blind to her faults, so when a friend made the hesitant suggestion that Shivka was "maybe a bit . . . willful," he answered, "Oh, she just likes *chachkas*. Toys. I can afford them, so why shouldn't I indulge her?" That beyond a certain point indulgence becomes a self-imposed slavery good for neither the slave nor the master he would not, could not see. He took each demand as it came, listened, obeyed, and cemented one more bar into the cage that was beginning to surround him.

Shortly thereafter the organ teacher came. He was a thin young man with a pencil moustache. He carried a set of silver-plated tools with which to adjust the innumerable interlocking levers, pedals, and enormous bronze pipes of the instrument, and a special rag to wipe its ivory keys, and another to wipe his gleaming black boots after he had dutifully accompanied Shivka Bellet on a philosophical walk through the village. He was saying, "You see the tonal qualities of the different notes vary in sensual . . ." when he got so caught up in his monologue that the fop stepped straight into the largest mound of horse dung in Proszowice; his boot sunk to the ankle.

The afternoon market crowd burst into peals of laughter. It wasn't the manure, for Poland was an agricultural country and everyone's shoes were similarly coated, but the look of absolute horror on the insipid young man's face. I am certain that could he have cut off his leg at the knee at that second he would willingly have done so. Instead he pulled an embroidered hanky from his breast pocket and dabbed vainly at the sticky waste, while the communal howls redoubled.

Shivka Bellet turned red with humiliation. "Stop that!" she snapped at her pet, then redirected her fury to the crowd. "How dare you . . . how dare you!" she sputtered, then slammed Isaac the Millionaire over the head with her furled parasol, jabbed it into the Doctor's paunchy gut, and dispersed the rest of us like a hurricane scatters a pile of dead leaves.

This was the calm before the storm. Events, which had begun with the eruption in the square, or maybe with Shivka's first sight of a three-color picture of the organ at Chartres, or maybe long before that, were not about to subside.

Hirsh David Bellet left his house one morning in a daze. Nobody knew what had occurred, but the pale face of the organist peered out the window after him and Shivka was locked in her room. People greeted the mogul; he walked in a trance. He went to his factory, his industrial sanctuary. Production was down and the wolves at bay.

"Work! Work!" he yelled.

One of the men said, "We won't work anymore until you buy us an organ," and Hirsh David lifted his hand to strike the man. Blood flowed down his arm, across his shoulder, into his brain. A vessel had burst. He fell dead on the floor.

Without a husband to torture, Shivka Bellet's life was empty. She sent the insignificant young organist back to Cracow like so much dirty laundry and allowed the tall bronze pipes to become clogged with dust and cobwebs. She was wealthy, but just as H.D.'s money had failed to satisfy her before he died, so it continued to fail.

The village matchmaker was so stimulated by the thought of a rich widow that he ignored Shivka's temperament. Alas, the intended partners did not. Even the toughest, homeliest, loneliest bachelor turned tail at the mention of this human dragon. Even Zalman the Digger had been approached. Sitting with a spade in his hand, basking in the autumn sun on the sanctified ground beyond the wrought-iron gates of the Proszowice cemetery, he listened quietly to the matchmaker's sales pitch. Then he commented on the uniquely bright shade of green above H. D. Bellet's grave, saying, "It's as if he's glad to be there."

There were times when most of us would gladly have changed places with Hirsh David to escape the black widow's wrath. She fought with the greengrocer over whether he should charge her for the extra leaves of lettuce, with the butcher over untrimmed fat, with anyone over anything. Her fury, we realized, had actually been tempered by the existence of Hirsh David, so that now her eyes flashed a brilliant gypsy indigo, her lips snarled in a carmine slash. Her tiny bust aquiver, hips swathed in armored brocade, she lashed out with the whip of her vitriolic tongue in every direction. She might have been pathetic if she hadn't been so vicious. Whenever she came to town, half of the stores pretended to close for the day, and even this didn't stop her. She stood outside, kicking the doors and cursing until we had no choice but to slink out of hiding and welcome her with a cheerful "Hello, so good to see you. Do come in."

All this false courtesy merited it received. "How dare you shut on a Tuesday morning? People depend on you. You have a responsibility," she ranted in my father's store, and so I was sent to placate her with a bowl of Mediterranean figs.

For a second her grimace softened, but then it reset, and she complained, "These are dry," and threw the entire expensive bowlful outside, where they sat in the dust by the doorway like pebbles. There was something about the configuration of orange spots on a magic beige carpet that evoked an oasis in the desert, but all they attracted was a stray dog that lived behind our house and ate whatever he could scavenge from our garbage, which rarely meant figs. Dry or not, they were a treat of the first order. He wolfed the first one down, savored another, and by his third fig had settled like a small, hairy sphinx in the doorway.

Now although I would never have favored the mangy freeloader with any such delicacy, once he had the figs I would not take them back, but I didn't know what to expect from Shivka Bellet. For the animal's own good I waved my hands at him to pack his treasure and scram, but all the silly mongrel did was stand up, lick my hands, and sit back down to his fruity repast.

Shivka Bellet had meanwhile berated my father for the terrible quality of everything he sold and for the terrible way in which he displayed his terrible merchandise, and I could tell that his patience was wearing thin and he was about to tell the grieving widow exactly where she could take her business, when she decided to take it there herself, spun around in her usual huff, and noticed the canine feasting. Surely, I thought, she was going to bite one of his perky furry ears off, but—miracle of miracles—she fairly gushed, "My, what a cute puppy!"

In unashamed response, the dog rolled over in the dirt and offered her his flea-bitten chest, which was taken into the immaculately talcumed hand. His tail was whipping up a cloud of dust, but Shivka Bellet, kneeling beside the dumb cur, paid it no heed and continued to scratch past the visible ribs to the taut drum of hungry dogbelly. "What's his name?" she asked.

"He doesn't really have one, Ma'am."

Her elegant fingers still lingering in the matted clumps of doggy hair, she turned sharply to me. "Are you being fresh?"

"No, definitely not," I hastened to reassure her, and to explain.

"We-e-ll then," she drawled until the conclusion to the sentence dawned on her in a revelation, "if he's a homeless puppy now, he shan't be for long. Come now, Adam," she added. God alone, blessed be He, knows where she got that name from, unless it had something   do with figs, their leaves, and the first man. "You," she said to i. e, "bring a pound, no, two pounds of *those*," she pointed regally at the figs, and then, as an afterthought, she crooked a finger at me, "and come along."

The carriage had pulled up beside our door and the newly named Adam scampered up the steps and inside as if he were accustomed to no less. I followed. In fact, I was hired on the spot to come every day to the large house on the outskirts of town to feed, play with, and basically continue to follow Adam.

We developed quite a rapport, myself and the mutt. The zloty a week Shivka Bellet was paying me was as princely a sum for a twelve-year-old as figs were food for a hound, so both he and I had benefited from her sudden generosity. Companions in benign roguery, we strolled about, Adam sniffing and scratching while I pondered the lack of reasons for our good fortune, each of us glancing now and then at the other, as if to say, "How lucky we are!"

Whatever the virtues of freedom, Adam was willing to surrender them in order to loll back on the velvet sofa H. D. Bellet had imported from Vienna. As much as she had previously demanded from her husband, Shivka Bellet delivered all that and more to her pet dog. He slept on Oriental carpets and ate from vases. He wore special doggie clothes sent from Cracow, including four tiny red rubber boots, so that he would not soil his delicate paws in the rain. He strutted about my father's store as a privileged customer, sure that whatever he sniffed at would be instantly wrapped, packed, and sent ahead to await his dining pleasure. His stomach grew so that it dragged along the ground and strangers mistook him for a pregnant bitch that was about to drop puppies any second, but we knew that the enormous pot was the result of Bobover's butchery and my father's creamed herring—and figs.

But as much as Adam took from the grande dame in the big house, he gave in return—at first. His transformation from scruffy vagabond to dashing hound-of-the-world paled before Shivka's change from harridan to gentlewoman. The burden imposed on her by her late husband's fortune weighed more easily when she had something to lavish it upon. This beneficence began to spread as she invited women of the town to lunch. She still remained aloof but not haughty, more like someone with a secret, which, of course, she was the only one to consider a secret. Every time Adam entered the room her complexion lit up in a delighted blush. He was the young hussar sweeping the contessa off her noble feet—while standing squarely on all four of his own.

A new life came to the house along with Adam. Gloomy, shuttered halls were reopened, the windows cleaned, floors waxed, furniture polished. Even the great organ was resurrected, and the public was invited to hear guest artists play beautiful music, during which Shivka would shed a tear of remorse for her past incivilities. After the recitals there were buffets, during which it was my job to keep an eye on the unacknowledged guest of honor. I had to intuit whether Adam would prefer the red or the black caviar, with or without a dab of cream cheese, or a pimento, or one of his modest old favorites, a fig. I almost forgot, as he may have and Shivka certainly did, that despite his personality and taste Adam was still a dog. As for the Proszowicer, they heartily approved of the changes he had wrought in his mistress but could not remember this awkward truth. The cur proved them right. He nosed about among the small mountain of wraps placed on the couch, found one he liked (Mrs. Horowitz's new magenta shawl), and promptly lifted his leg.

The hearty chime of the organ pealed forth.

Once again it was Zalman the Digger who voiced our distress. "And if you're not buried in the shade," he said, "you're buried in the sun," and he lifted his hoe and set to work trimming the edges of Hirsh David's plot.

Who knows how character changes? As Shivka Bellet gradually gained a youthful charm, the object of her affections assumed her former spleen. Adam became the same spoiled child of luxury that she had after her marriage, and the more she slaved for him the less he appreciated it. He ripped the stuffing from the sofa out of sheer pique and was always ready to use the weapon he had discovered in his bladder. He grew coarse and snappish—that is, when he wasn't as lazy as a slug. His cheery yelp became a raucous bark that grated through nights of willful disrespect. The difference between a request and a command is evident even in a dog's limited vocabulary, and Adam was no ordinary dog. He was more like a demon.

I was walking to Shivka Bellet's house. I could see it at the bend in the road that leads toward Cracow and the rest of the world. Shivka herself was silhouetted in the doorway like a saint in a church niche. Frantic with apprehension, she was crying, "Adam! Here, boy, come here, boy! A-a-a-adam!"

But that dog wasn't going to come or go anywhere. He lay beside the gate at the edge of Shivka's property, gathering flies. "Adam?" I asked. "Are you dead?" He still had a smirk on his face, as if he were dreaming of juicy Mediterranean figs. I lifted him, lighter by the weight of a soul than he had been a day before, and carried him forward, like an offering for the shattered altar of love.

Would that anyone but me had had this awful responsiblity! The cold, limp flesh scared me, and so did the thought of Shivka Bellet's hot-blooded reaction. I need not have feared. As soon as she saw my one-man funeral procession, she grew quiet. Her worst imaginings come true, she steeled herself to face them. She took Adam in her arms and then said to me, "Inform Zalman."

By the time I got to town the news had preceded me. Mouth to ear to mouth to ear, word spread with the rapidity of flight. I was called to from the porch of Jergenchic the barber for verification, but I had been entrusted with a mission and could not stop to satisfy mere curiosity. Moreover, I did not want to stop to think.

It was a relief to find Zalman napping under the single yew tree on the cemetery grounds, amid the pale marble forest from which no leaf ever falls. I was strangely excited by the Digger's ignorant peace. I had the sense of being with something larger than myself, and the tragedy I had come to relate was overwhelmed by the terrible thrill. I hastened to blurt out the news.

But all Zalman said was, "Whatever she wishes."

I was a human pendulum, swinging one way through the town to the cemetery and then back to Shivka Bellet. The thought that my employment might terminate with my companion's demise had never occurred to me. No matter how minor, I was a participant in the onrush of events, and I would see them through to whatever conclusion they prefaced.

Shivka Bellet was sitting quietly in her rocking chair. She was wearing the same mourning dress she had worn for her husband and was staring vacantly through the lead-paned window onto the backyard lawn where Hirsh David had often eaten his breakfast and Adam his lunch, where she herself had spent some of the kindest and cruelest moments of her life. She turned her ashen face to me and said, "I will need you for one more day. I will pay you well."

The servant ushered me out of the room into another, where I was hastily fitted with appropriate mourner's garb. (I think it was one of H. D. Bellet's old suits hacked off and hemmed at the knees, its waist simply bunched and sewn, and it fit no better than a burlap bag.) In this ludicrous attire I was sent back to accompany Shivka in her grief.

She was rocking monotonously, her eyes locked on some point in the distance, away from the white silk sheet that enwrapped the body. For hours we sat in eerie, almost religious transfixion before the bier of the dead animal, yet I was surprised when a gas lantern flamed on because it was dark. Then the servant announced, "It is time, Madam."

Although it was obviously she who, in a more lucid moment, had dictated the procedures we were to follow, Shivka hardly seemed to know where she was. She nodded her head, an obedient child, and stepped into her carriage, while the servant and I placed Adam on her lap and then climbed up together to the driver's seat. I was consumed by curiosity, but remained solemn and decided to wait until we arrived wherever the team's easy canter was taking us. Moonlight filtered through the clouds, giving the impression that we were under water. Dust rose behind us and settled along the deserted main street of Proszowice. Not a soul was anywhere; there was no trace of the gossip that would have swamped us mere hours ago. The trees, just beginning to lose their leaves, revealed a fantastic inner structure like ribs seen through starved skin.

I should have realized that it was just the next swing of the pendulum we were riding, delayed but inevitable. The cemetery gates looked like enormous, half-melted wax candles. I couldn't remember if they were usually locked, but there was no lock on them now, and we pushed them open and entered. Zalman the Digger's hut was quiet. The only sounds were the snuffling of the horses, the crunching of pebbles underfoot, and the whispers of the dead. Their tombs were glowing like glass bricks, murmuring of sacrilege, or maybe welcome. I supposed that it would depend on whether it was the friendly street puppy or the hostile house dog that joined them on the other side.

I did not know if the grave had been dug for some child to be buried on the morrow or if it was the start of a grave for a grown man or if one grave was always kept half-dug in morbid anticipation, but there it was, a small hole with not more than a wheelbarrow's-worth of dirt heaped beside it. A shovel stuck up from this mound like a marker.

Shivka Bellet's arms were wrapped securely around the enshrouded animal as if it were a swaddled babe. She stood at the head of the grave, a black apparition in the moonlight, unmoving as we gently coaxed from her the tragic burden. We laid the dog as softly as we could on the cold, unyielding earth. The tail slipped free of its silken enclosure, and I imagined for a moment that it wagged. For the first time I felt sorry for Adam. I also felt sorry for Shivka and for myself and for the many outraged dead who surrounded us. I felt an all-embracing sorrow that my heart could barely contain.

Then, as if rising in hollow reverberation from the depths, from the direction of Hirsh David Bellet's magnificent stone came the prayer for the dead. *Yisgadal, vayiskaddash*—"Magnified and sanctified be the great name of God throughout the world which He hath created according to His will. May He establish His kingdom during the days of your life and during the life of all the house of Israel, speedily, yea, soon; and say ye, Amen."

Like iron to a magnet, I muttered the traditional response: "May His great name be blessed for ever and ever."

The voice (it was Zalman the Digger's) continued while Shivka and I stood with our heads bowed in mute respect. The entire prayer took only a minute, until it concluded, "May He who establisheth peace in the heavens grant peace unto us and unto all Israel; and say ye, Amen."

"Amen."

Then Zalman emerged from the dark necropolis and began to shovel the dirt over the luxurious silk shroud. As each spadeful obscured another patch of white, Shivka progressively stiffened until she was like a marble angel in a Christian cemetery. She remained immobile as Zalman handed the shovel to me, and I cast a ritual clod of earth into the disappearing vault. She remained immobile as Zalman held out the shovel one last time.

I had never seen him as other than the laconic, misshapen Digger, but now, as master of this bizarre ceremony, Zalman was implacable. He scooped the remaining clods of earth onto the gray metal crescent of the shovel, but still he thrust it grimly forward, as if offering a choice of weapons to a dueling partner. They both stood in frozen tableau, the spirits of the yard circling and howling with the wind.

From her savagery to her misery, this woman had been the epitome of strength. She trembled but stood fast: but Zalman stood faster. Finally Shivka, a pitiful shade of her former self, was forced to accept the responsibility. She exchanged one look of infinite pain with Zalman. Then she reached out her quivering white palms and let the dirt sift slowly off the edge of the shovel back whence it had come.

PART II

Proszowice was a town of talkers. Rhapsodic, romantic, pedantic, crooning or kvetching, crying or kibitzing, everyone was endlessly engaged in this one pursuit. From the moment we woke from the mute prison of our dreams, we were discussing the night before, anticipating the day to come, exulting in the moment at hand. We praised, slandered, affirmed, and denied with equal good cheer. We told stories and fables and outright lies, which our friends had the grace not to question. We talked to each other, to ourselves, and, when no one else would listen, to the Great Listener in the sky, blessed be He—to God. "And in the beginning was the Word."

Silence was automatically suspect. It was considered arrogant, enigmatic; worst of all, it was private. We felt as if we had a right to each other's pains and pleasures. The notion of the individual was anathema to that of community. I remember Selma Rabinovitch telling my mother that silence caused ulcers: "You know, the juices, they just sit and turn sour."

If this was true, then I feared for my stomach. Yes, I must admit that I was one of the few who held their tongues. If talk gave our town substance, then I was a shadow beside the public body, a dwarfish gray darkness touching, yet never quite one with, the Proszowicer. There was something mysterious that bound us together, but, like sound, it evaded my childish grasp. When the babble and squawk grew too great, I sought retreat, asylum.

In my family's house, however, there were always younger siblings tumbling around me. With these cubs ever-present, how could I think sensitive thoughts?

In my father's store there was worse: work. The volatile connection I sensed would never come while I was slicing herring and scooping their insides into a barrel of bloody seepage.

So I went to my grandmother's house. Sunlit through a dark yellow shade, filled with overstuffed, worn velvet chairs and a plethora of cast bronze and ceramic knickknacks and pictures in gilt and morocco frames, it was a mystical cave that kindled the imagination—which the old lady herself promptly doused. Hunched over a kettle she was stirring with a long wooden spoon, she sampled it noisily, wrinkled her face like a monkey's, then turned to me and said, "So. So that pistachio of yours, she still plays with the gentile machines?"

"I don't understand, Grandma."

"Ptah. Like nobody else ever lost any love. Think's she's Joan Sebastian Martyr. So why did you stop with the violin?"

I understood that she was mixing up Shivka's organ, Shivka's widowhood, her own widowhood, and my own late, unlamented musical career. So I fled from the last haven I had. I roamed the streets, avoiding both horse droppings and human noise with instinctive deftness. I skirted the market with its haggling, the mikvah with its gossip, the shul with its prayers, the hushed intimacies of lovers in doorways, the hysterics of solitary madmen. But I could not escape. The words of others surrounded me.

In the meantime I crossed the village square, my head burdened with the many puzzles that beset me. I passed the church spire and the Proszoworks smokestack; I forgot where I was going, if anywhere. Mulling, wondering, I walked a straight line, the clamor within me increasing even as it dwindled without. I kicked pebbles eastward, so abstracted that my blind pacing took me out of town— straight up to, or into, something that cracked my tender head. The gates blurred. Zalman the Digger was hovering over me, a dirty, stooping angel against a background of pale blue sky.

For a second I wondered if I was dead, maybe run over by an ox cart; but I could feel the sun on my face. My eyes focused on Zalman's rough palms wrapped around the simple horizontal gate latch, and, I don't know why, but I said, "There's no lock," as if that were the reason I had walked into it, trying to butt the thing open, like a goat.

"Why should there be? . . . We allow everybody in." He helped me to my feet and escorted me through a field of tombstones, their letters faded, their shoulders rounded. I felt as if I were in synagogue, walking down the aisle to pray between the old men.

Zalman had a small hut in the corner of the cemetery. It contained one neatly made bed, a miniature stove over which a few cooking implements were hanging on nails rusted by rising steam, and a carpentry shop. This consisted of a long table crowded with hammers and saws and other esoteric tools, and with glass jars filled with different-sized nails and other tiny metal things. Stacks of wood were lined up against the wall underneath it, in order of size. Zalman took a rag, dipped it into a barrel of rainwater, and touched it to my forehead, where it stung, then soothed. I shut my eyes and let the cool wetness draw the pain out of me.

For as long as I could remember, Zalman had been the Digger. He might well have sprung from the sandy cemetery ground a thousand years ago, might well have buried the first Jewish Proszowicer, might well stay to bury the last, and to exhume us on the Day of Judgment, rapping at our moldering coffins with his long shovel handle, calling, "Wake up! Wake!" . . . he was calling softly.

I jumped, my hand slapping down on the scratchy woolen blanket. I had had a vision of something grand, but it was lost in the confines of the smoky hovel. I tried to reach backward into my prophetic memory of the glorious kingdom beneath the ground.

"It's time to go home."

"I passed out."

"You have a very nasty bump."

I put my hand to my head, which swelled to meet the groping fingers. The bump throbbed, but as I rubbed it the throbbing lessened, and so did my many anxieties. I looked into Zalman's compassionate brown eyes. He was the only one in the whole town who wouldn't be oohing and ahhing and recounting the time he hit his head or how King Solomon once hit his head or how the Warsaw train once derailed or how I should be pleased because at least this proved that I *had* a head. No, Zalman sat beside me on a three-legged footstool, saying nothing because he had nothing to say, and that alone comforted me more than any chatty sympathy. I remembered Zalman's midnight prayer for the soul of the dog, Adam, and I felt a sense of pervasive calm, of the peace that had so long eluded me. This was the shelter I had been seeking. Before I left I asked the Digger, "May I come back?"

"I'm sure you will," he said, and it wasn't until I was halfway home that a shudder ran down my spine when the delayed realization of his double meaning came to me.

Well aware of my destination, I did return to the spooky holy grounds a day later. I let myself in and stood in the midst of the palpable quiet, afraid to disturb those who rested there, whose names were carved in the corners of my vision. There was my father's grandfather and my mother's grandparents and the families of my friends and Isaac the Millionaire's wives and the unmarked rectangle that belonged to the dog Adam and the many others whose memories were gone the way of their materiality. Then I heard a harsh, unnatural rasp.

Zalman lived with the dead. Whether it was this that made him silent or whether his silence had led him to do so, I never knew. No one had ever heard him laugh.

The rasp came again, then more rapidly, and I identified it and smiled at my fears. It was the sound of a saw, and it was coming from inside Zalman's cabin. I made out the golden haze of sawdust flying upward and the bent shape of the carpenter creating this whirlwind. His body was hunched over, his arm pumping violently, as the teeth of the saw bit deeper, cried louder, until an abrupt snap split the remaining board in two.

The motes of sawdust began to settle like snowflakes on Zalman's shoulders. He flipped over the six-foot length of wood, clamped it into his vise, and took a plane to it. There was a clicking sound as the plane picked off splinters left by the saw. Curls of blonde pine accumulated on the floor like hair at a barber's feet.

Zalman began to sand his board. The sheet of grainy emery he used made an incongruously gentle sound, as smooth as its effect on the wood. I sat under the yew tree beside the cabin, but now that I was finally in a position restful enough to muse, now of all times, I was seized by a desire to talk. "What are you making?"

Zalman had not yet shown any recognition of my presence, but he didn't miss a beat. "Coffins."

"Oh," I backed up against the yew tree. "How do you decide what size to make them?"

"The grain," he answered, and continued to work, cutting, planing, sanding, then joining with swift blows of the hammer. Only when the sun began to dip toward the horizon, when the flecks of wood still floating in the air were tinged with red, did Zalman lay down his tools and wipe his forehead with a blue speckled rag. I wiped my own forehead on the arm of my sleeve. Zalman filled a kettle with water and set it to boil. "Except, of course, when there's a specific order," he clarified.

"Why do you stay?"

His shoulders made an enormous circular shrug as if they were independent of the body beneath them.

I answered his gesture. "There are a million places you can go, a million things you can do. There's a whole world out there," I began to lecture, when the tea kettle spoke for my host, "Ssssh."

Zalman poured out two steaming cups of the acidic blend, then passed me a jar of golden honey. It gleamed in the twilight slanting through the open doorway, so that it seemed like a thing alive. I spooned some into my tea and sipped carefully; I waited.

At last, as if a vow of silence had come to an end, Zalman spoke. "When I was your age I felt that great things were meant for me if only I was prepared to grasp them when the opportunity came."

"Yes, exactly."

"I did not know what exactly these great things were to be, but I felt that they were nonetheless inevitable. I felt destiny slumbering within me. . . . Not that I was asleep. I was an excellent student, the first in my class, and was offered a scholarship to the yeshiva in Lublin. . . ." I could see him remembering the yeshiva, constructing the home of godly knowledge in his mind, brick by earthly brick. He said, "I think that was my first mistake."

"Going to Lublin?"

"Not going to Lublin. You see, there were so many scholars in Poland, and I thought that I was being readied for something that was not merely special but absolutely unique." Here Zalman lapsed into silence and fell asleep. He worked long hours and was unaccustomed to conversation, so both his labor and his speech had worn him out. I took the thin woolen blanket and covered him. Then I stood in the doorway and looked out over the field of stones and wondered what those who lay beneath them had expected for themselves and whether their expectations had been satisfied. These were easy thoughts, but they were true, and though I later found their form shallow, I have never denied their content. I plucked one of the last green leaves from the yew tree before I pushed open the creaky cemetery gate.

More leaves fell in the next few days. Zalman kept busy raking, then burning them in a smoldering pyre beside the coffin he was still working on, cutting, planing, sanding, joining, then staining and hinging. Except when the old women came to visit the markers of the men they had married, the children they had borne, the parents they still mourned, or, as Shivka Bellet did every Wednesday, her pet, and except for the buried men, women, children, and dog, we were alone.

"My life," Zalman said.

It was the first sound he had made since he had told me of his childhood dreams. I boiled the tea and spooned the beautiful honey into it and handed him the blue cup and kept the red for myself before he continued: "I could have been a soldier, a merchant, a musician. All of these opportunities offered themselves to me, and all of them I refused, for none of them was of sufficient . . . magnitude. I did not know what I was waiting for, but I could wait. That was my truly unique quality, but, of course, that was the one quality that no one could see. They could see my intelligence and my strength—forgive me for seeming immodest, but since I am no longer strong or intelligent I can speak thus—but they never saw what it took out of my soul to withstand the claims they made upon me. They never saw my patience."

"Yes. Yes."

"Wait," he told me, and went to sleep.

I came back the next day, overflowing. I told Zalman stories— funny stories and sad stories, about school and home, and secret stories that I had never told anyone else before—all to the single point that I wanted and desperately needed to comprehend what was going on around me. I had to know. I could not wait.

"Well," he sighed, and his uncertainty cut me like a knife. "I was made one final offer."

I imagined fabulous castles in mythological kingdoms, gold and glory.

"She was a little younger than I. She lived next door."

"Who?"

"She played in the front yard, so I saw her every day on my way to and from cheder. She hummed the melodies of the songs that I had been practicing on the piano. Sometimes I would tease her, and a solemn expression would cross her face before it relit with pleasure, and she would say, 'Yes, Zalman.'

"She was at my Bar Mitzvah. I remember that as I recited the words of my Haftorah and let my eyes scan the synagogue benches I saw her, silently mouthing the words along with me.

"It was assumed, even then, between my parents and her widowed mother, that we would marry. But as my worldly promise became evident, as I outstripped my classmates in both Talmud and wrestling, my parents began to think that I was too good for the girl next door. There was talk of betrothing me to the niece of a rich Cracow furrier. Oh, there were no limits to my future, but I knew that the girl was as worthy of me as I was of the honors to come." He lifted his palms, as if to feel the weight of the dismal shack. "Honors," he said.

Chances came and went, and Zalman continued to wait for his own personal miracle. His "promise" disappeared, and so did the big-city nieces, but his faith never wavered, and neither did that of the girl next door. Time passed. His patience begat nought but the need to be more patient.

Then the girl's mother took ill. Zalman went on: "A man offered to pay for an operation . . . *if* my friend would marry him. She had a dog. We walked it. We came here. Maybe we thought that by facing the ultimate inevitable we could stave off the day." He mused and gazed out over his macabre dominion as if the girl's dog of old were still romping among the tombs. "There were fewer stones then, maybe less moss, and the tree was smaller, but cemeteries never really change. . . . She said that if I could give her any hope, any hope whatsoever, she would spurn her fancy suitor to wed me.

"I told her of my destiny, of the great thing I expected to be or do, though I did not know what it was, or when it would come. I told her that I could not betray my patience, which told me to wait and keep waiting and wait forever if need be, and how until forever came I could not help her. I told her that I was terribly, terribly sorry, and that I did not expect her to believe me.

"'No,' she said, 'I believe, but I cannot wait. I . . . ' We kissed."

At the memory, Zalman's eyes closed. I began to tiptoe deferentially toward the door, but a strange voice interrupted my passage.

"It was the finest moment of my life."

Early next morning I saw Zalman's figure diligently at work. With measured stroke his back bent, his shovel plunged. He could not have started more than a half-hour before, at dawn, because the ground was hardly broken.

I hesitated by the wrought-iron threshold. I thought that the fence was a magic barrier beyond which I became invisible.

The scrape of the shovel continued like the ticking of a clock, and I stood mesmerized, feeling only a soft tugging of muscles in my shoulder and a slight queasiness as the pit sank lower and lower, as Zalman stepped into it and I saw his shovel arch out from it in order to deposit one more batch of earth, darker brown the farther down he dug.

After the girl had left him, other opportunities failed him too. When the old Digger died, Zalman took his place. It was just a temporary job, he thought; but there he was. "Here I am," he proclaimed. "Still waiting. So what grand fate lies in store for the humble Digger of Proszowice?"

"Why did you bury the dog Adam?"

"I will bury anyone."

"But why did you say Kaddish?"

"So that someone will say it for me."

We were in the shanty at sunset; gold and crimson over the fields was visible through the doorway. Tea was steeping, and a dreamy look suffused Zalman's face. "One never knows when the finest moment of one's life will come," he said, stripping off his sweat-stained flannel work clothes layer by layer until they made a ragged heap. Standing naked, a gaunt, gray-skinned philosopher, he said, "It could be a religious moment, in prayer." He scooped a right handful of water from the rain barrel and laved it across his left chest, shoulder, and arm, then repeated a mirror-image motion for the other half of his body. "It could be a moment in business or music," he said as he splashed water down on and between his legs, a puddle accumulating by his knobby toes. Scrubbing this face and chin, he told me, "It could be a sight, a smell, a taste," then submerged his entire head in the water, bubbled incomprehensibly, and rose to the surface, shaking himself like a dog. "Or a kiss," he said, looking down at the floor and rubbing himself dry with a rough purple towel.

I began to feel stifled and melancholy in the now damp cabin air. Zalman, however, was oblivious to my creeping distress. He seemed to have forgotten my very presence. He put on a shirt whiter than any I had ever seen him wear, and cleaner pants; yet the more respectable he looked, the more disturbing his appearance became. Finally he crowned himself with a knitted black skullcap, and suddenly said, "One chance for a lifetime of moments traded, for what? for the phantoms of the imagination, the horror, the calling, the spade with which to dig my own grave."

I struggled against the evil intuitions crowding upon me and managed to ask, "Why are you telling me this?"

"I take walks," he said. "At night. I see things that no one else does. Once I saw you playing the violin. I used to be a musician; I played the piano, and the organ. I thought you knew."

"I know nothing!" I cried, avoiding the awful convergences I had sought, the thought of which I could no longer abide.

Zalman resumed his monologue. "I have waited all my life. It has been my single virtue. I have one more wait to endure," he said, then instructed, "When it is over, please cover me, but ...," and here he addressed me for the first time as myself rather than as servant or confidant, "but ...," he gave me his considered advice, "don't take the job"—as if I might.

Without a backward glance he strode out the door. I scrambled to follow him, but it seemed to take eons to get my legs moving in that lonely place, oppressed by the lifetime of unlived moments that Zalman had spent there. By the time I caught up with him he was across the yard; stepping carefully down into the grave he had dug, he lay down in the coffin he had made.

"But . . ." my voice was snuffed like a candle by the lid closing. He was gone. I was alone, with only the spirits of my people to accompany me in the vigil assigned me. I yearned to talk to them, to tell them of the fear and sadness I felt, not for death, but for the tragedy called life that precedes it. But they would speak only to each other, just as Shivka and Zalman the Digger had the night we buried Adam. I overheard a joke I could not understand rustling through the yew tree. It carried off a few shriveled leaves, as if it knew there was no longer anyone to rake them. The hovel in the corner looked a hundred years abandoned. The whole cemetery, which had become so familiar to me, seemed suddenly foreign. Still, I remained, and let the sounds of the dead wash me. As I looked down at the enormous wooden box at the bottom of the grave, I thought of the search for peace that had brought me here, and of how little I had done about it, just as Zalman had done so little with his infinite patience.

A wall of dusk was descending, crushing the last glimmer of colored light in the west. Unwilling to push my luck into the night, I freed the shovel from the mound beside me and began the prayer for the dead. *Yisgadal, vayiskaddash*—"Magnified and sanctified be the great name of God throughout the world, which He hath created according to His will. . . ." My voice was small in the face of the oncoming dark. It cracked, a twig in the forest. I felt young and ignorant, and most of all alone, until I finished the prayer and said "Amen"—and there was an echo.

"Amen!"

There was only one place it could have come from. My shovel poised, partially in defense, I leaned forward. "Zalman?" I called into the meter-deep abyss. "Zalman, are you still alive?"

"Throw the dirt for God's sake!" he cried, then hastened to add, "blessed be He."

I put the shovel down. "I can't do that."

With a weary creak, the coffin lid opened. Only a fast-fading ray of light penetrated the nocturnal shadows, but Zalman blinked his eyes like someone staring at the sun, habituating himself to the idea of release from the absolute dark to which he had consigned himself.

"There, there," I comforted him. "It just wasn't time for you to meet your destiny."

"When?" he asked.

"I don't know," I answered, and reached to help him out.

Ventriloquism

ometimes my thoughts were like fish. Evasive, obscure, deep. But when they rose to the surface I could reach into the pool of myself and spear them. I could extract them, examine them, peel off the glittering scales, remove the bones, devour the meat. Still, the essence of the creature was withheld from me. The fish out of water was as desolate as a starving child, its stupefied expression one of lack.

It was a quiet day, not long after my first expeditions into the outside world had come to their various, dismal ends. I had retreated from the zone of the imagination to the borders of everyday life: I played; I prayed; I ate my mother's *chulent*. The only remnants of my unconventional past were my walks. Like a hunter lost in the woods who inclined to one foot, I traveled in long, aimless circles, although sometimes I walked straight until the weather changed, and sometimes in patterns like pentacles or Jewish stars. I trod my worries into the fertile Polish earth. It was not the specifically thoughtful nature of these walks but the random thoughts they engendered, like fish, that I appreciated. I was beside the river, under my favorite tree, when a voice hailed me. "Well, boy."

Aside from someone asleep in the grass ten meters downstream, nobody else was in sight. I scanned the far banks, which were bare, when the voice repeated, "Well, since when don't you say hello?"

Was Moshele Rosen playing a trick on me? I glanced quickly into the knothole. I craned my neck up to peer into the dense green overgrowth. A nesting blue warbler flew away. Behind me I heard, "Yoo hoo!" I spun around before the voice faded. Nevertheless, again behind me, "Psst."

Like a horse whipped, I ran. I was in mid-leap, hurdling the figure in the grass, when he cried, "Here I am!" and his voice tripped me like a log.

"Watch it, fat feet," he scolded me, although he was scarcely larger than an infant. Maybe he was a dwarf. Dressed in baggy pants and a checked shirt, a sailor's cap covering most of his red head, he moved no more than a stone.

"I'm sorry," I said. "I said, I'm sorry, but I was scared.... Excuse me." I nudged him. He flipped. He was a rag doll with no joints, no muscles, no substance beneath his enormous head. His eyes were blue marbles, his nose a carved hook, his mouth locked in a permanent grin in a square wooden jaw. Then his chin literally dropped, revealing his square wooden teeth, and a windy moan bade, "Pick me up."

I obeyed.

"Scratch my back," he demanded. "Don't be shy now, under the shirt. A little lower. There. Ahhh, there," he sighed as I put my hand into his hollow interior. My fingers explored eagerly in the darkness until I found that my thumb and pinky could control his arms, my middle fingers the hinges of a mouth. I plucked a string.

"Oh ho! that tickles ... Fresh!" He slapped me with his limp left hand.

"Who are you?" I asked him.

"Air to a fortune."

"Where are you from?"

"Wood that you knew."

"How old are you?"

"As old as my teeth, as young as your tongue. Or vice versa."

"What is your name?"

He refused to answer. His eyelids, brittle, translucent shells, closed, and he slept. Contrary to his harsh, riddling character, he was like a baby in my arms. Breezes from the river tickled the tall grass. A wrinkled leaf drifted down from the ancient oak. My weightless burden's comic face reflected the last, angling rays of the sun.

"Well," I yawned with deliberate exaggeration, "I have to leave now. It's time for my dinner," but only a snore curled out from his pursed mouth in response. "Are you going to sleep here? It may rain. You'll be cold, you'll warp." I hesitated, then decided to follow my charitable impulse. "Would you like to come home with me? ... There's plenty of room."

He opened one eye. "I thought you'd never ask." He winked.

Fully awake, if he had ever really been asleep, my companion hummed a jolly tune. His pitch was off, as if his vocal chords were made of wax paper, but his energy was unflagging. His arms swung vehemently as I carried him, and sometimes they rose to conduct an invisible orchestra. By the time we came to the small hillock that offered a panoramic view of Proszowice, he was blaring loudly "Yiddle, biddle, boom, boom," and flinging his straw-stuffed arms and legs in all directions. Perhaps a hundred mean dwellings spread beneath us in irregular radiation from the town square.

"For this you interrupted me?" he snorted, and kept on singing.

I admit that I had my own doubts about the benefits of village life, but it was OK for me to be ungrateful: I lived there. I refrained, however, from chiding my guest and brought him down from the knoll into the town, where I assumed he would feel more at home. Unfortunately he did, like a bantam cock in the roost.

The first people we saw were the Rabbi and the Doctor. With his somber overcoat and vast black beard, the Rabbi looked like a shaggy bear, while the Doctor, in beige linen and steel-rimmed glasses, was the visible embodiment of enlightenment. They were deep in an endless secular/sectarian dispute. "Even your damned, evoluting science admits that it has no basis, no first cause," the Rabbi argued.

Before the Doctor could answer, my new acquaintance jumped in. "Godmonger!" he hooted. "Faith-baiting, spirit-stripping, holy racketeer!"

I was shocked.

In the course of his many years of disagreement with the Rabbi the Doctor often boiled over, but he believed in the Lord, blessed be He, and he tried to perform the 613 mitzvahs to the best of his ability. He would never, ever, under any circumstances, say anything disrespectful. He couldn't believe his ears. "What?" He turned around.

"You shut up, four eyes!"

"What?" Now the Rabbi turned around.

"Nothing," I stammered. "I . . . I . . . I said it was cloudy, rain later, spring showers, snow maybe. . . . To sum up, more nice . . . weather we should have . . . God willing."

"Dog killing."

I clamped my ill-mannered cohort's mouth shut until we escaped. But the rest of our short journey was no better. He outraged and insulted everyone we saw. He was an arrogant, abusive bully. He harped on physical defects (yelling, "March. Two. Sree. Feir!" at crippled Mrs. Hemtobble); and when he could find none, he just lied. His lies, however, had the element of truth that made them vicious, as if he knew everybody's secret weakness. For example, he bowed with hyperbolic politeness to Mrs. Horowitz and her three unmarried daughters, saying, "What lovely girls, but such bad chess players!"

Neither I nor the Horowitzes understood.

He explained. "Because they never mate."

And don't ask what he said to Isaac the Millionaire.

He didn't know when to stop. Yet the worst was still to come. His head turned one hundred and eighty degrees on its axis and he leered up at me. I had the spookiest feeling that he could read my mind. I was thinking that I obviously could not take him to dinner with my family, but neither could I disengage myself from my invitation. "Well," I said, my heart sinking, "Here we are."

"Home sweet hovel." He had no mercy.

"This is our store," I said as I pushed open the front door.

He surveyed the ceiling-high shelves crammed full of merchandise, the jars and display cases, the barrels of herring. "Goods for the gods, eh?" he sneered, and let one arm dangle and splash the pickle brine as we passed by. "Smell this, fish face."

Luckily, nobody in the kitchen noticed as we stepped past. My father was engrossed in study, my mother, in stirring the pot. My brother and sister were on the floor amid a clutter of building blocks and stuffed animals. They must have heard me upstairs though, because the second I opened the door to my room my mother announced, "Dinner in five minutes."

"Nice closet," my new friend said. "Where's the room?"

Of course it was small, and probably seemed smaller due to the three beds and dressers it contained. Of course it was common, its quilts threadbare, its wallpaper peeling, but like the rest of the house, and the rest of the town, it adequately fulfilled our simple needs.

"Look," I pointed out, "You were sleeping under a tree when we met."

"Ah, the great outdoors, the fresh air, the freedom!"

"The cold, the damp!"

"I miss it already."

"As far as I'm concerned you can go right back there," and I stepped to the window.

"NO!" he shrieked, and one little hand clutched at the jamb. His four fingers were carved from a single piece of wood, the thumb in opposition. His arm was rigid. He squeezed, and a crack burst across the clear pane like lightning. "You're a great one for discarding, aren't you? One hitch and it's out the window. You expect me to go quietly? Forget it! What do you think I am— some bloody violin?"

His grip may have been inflexible, but mine wasn't. I dropped him on the bed and staggered back from the broken window. "How do . . . ?" I knew I shouldn't argue. I knew I couldn't win. But I didn't know when to stop. "That's different," I said, attempting to justify myself in a situation where any justification would be twisted into a self-accusation.

"Uh huh, uh huh, uh huh, uh huh . . . ," he continued, until I pulled the blanket over him, wishing I were a magician who could make him disappear.

"Hey, pally," he addressed me from the shroud, "give my apologies downstairs. I'm not such a big eater, but you, pally, you can eat for two, can't you?"

I nearly tripped over the crease in the faded gray runner. The banister creaked as I swung around its globe-topped post and flung myself into the far chair that had been mine for as long as I could remember. Everyone else was already seated. My father was in the middle of the blessing for bread. "Amen," I said, and grabbed a hunk, which tore off in a shower of crumbs.

I tried to enjoy the meal, but the absent guest spoiled it for me. How did he know about the violin, about Isaac the Millionaire? How could he hint at the Yom Kippur feast that was strictly between me and my bad conscience? How could he infiltrate himself into my very guts? I felt a series of ominous rumblings coming from the region of my stomach. "Grrr," they seemed to say. "Grapes?" I wondered. I would stuff them into him, where they would ferment, run into wine, and seep through to stain the lines in his jaw.

"Grr. Niblck. Systv." "Gravy?" maybe. Never before had I felt the functions of my stomach so vividly. I imagined it as a cave dotted with pools of steaming chicken soup where noodles floated like eels. Vapors rose and dissipated among the potato-pudding stalactites. There were pot-roast walls with gravy springs, all feeding the antagonistic power within me. He growled threateningly, but the sound was muffled by the rest of my body.

My brother put his head to my stomach to listen to the drips, drizzles, burbles, and gleeps. "It sounds like the old men praying," he remarked, before I pushed him angrily aside. He looked hurt, but I could not contend with sensitive familial issues; a monster was squirming through my intestinal tract, climbing over my liver, and jumping up and down on my spleen until I could not help but cry out, "Great heavens!"

My mother bent solicitously toward me. "What's the matter?" she asked. "Would you like some more soup?"

I intended to smile at her maternal cure-all but must have grimaced instead, because she leaned back in alarm. I felt the terrrible urge to say something insolent. Upstairs, I could hear the faint janglings of the intruder in my bed.

"What's that?" my brother said.

There had been nothing fundamentally wrong about my actions. My father often invited those less fortunate than we home for Shabbos dinner. It was the particular individual I had had the bad judgment to invite that caused the problem. I was terrified of what he might reveal. One thing I did not need was a vindictive inquisitor tossing in bed and turning my stomach.

"It sounds like an animal."

"Probably squirrels in the attic."

"I'll check," I said, and dashed from the kitchen, knowing that they were looking after me, shrugging their shoulders, saying without words, "He's at it again."

"Ersnapatum. Vskler. Rdbdbdb." The churning gurgling scared me. I tensed in apprehension of disaster and set both my hands to kneading my midsection to stave off some violent internal combustion, but it was as helpful as trying to cap a volcano. I collapsed on my bed curled into a trembling, fetal question mark. I sweated and shivered, and alternately let one hand glide off my belly to seek warmth between my legs while the other wound out from under the blue quilt for cool fresh air. I dared not turn to my bed's other occupant. I could imagine his mouth like fire full of teeth like icecubes.

Although I didn't think more than a minute had elapsed, I heard my brother enter. I heard his prayers and my mother's distinctive footsteps, like the patter of rain. "Ssssh, kinder," she whispered. "Your brother is sickly. Good night." I felt her kiss on my forehead, like rain.

This gentle compassion threw me into an irrational rage. I seethed and felt the bile rising inside me like lava, but all I said was, "Glstle. Mirch."

Then, from the dark beside me, there was an echo. "Lshkv. Prshkv." It was my unwelcome guest, playing games, having a high old time. There I was in pain while the object of my ill-advised benevolence mocked me. The worst of it was that the more he aped me, the more my stomach ached in sympathetic distress.

I told him to shut up. At least I began to tell him. I coughed up phlegm and worked my jaw, but merely gave rise to a heavy breath. Only the sounds of his crude burlesque of my suffering were audible. "Crsk. Llk. Ysky." I tried again, placing my teeth on my lip, guiding my tongue to my palate, manipulating the muscles of my throat, but . . . nothing. It was as if I had forgotten some basic part of the speechifying process that one ordinarily does instinctively. It had never occurred to me that speaking was a skill, that more than will was needed in order to achieve tone, timbre, voice. In frustration, I slammed my hand down to jolt myself back to a sound mind. Instead it knocked on a hard, wooden surface.

"Who's there?"

Then I realized. He had stolen my voice.

The crack in the window cast a shadow across the bed like a broken sword. There was dust in the air and a scratching in the eaves, probably squirrels. I could not remonstrate; I could not beg; I could not talk. I turned and reached for the snake-thin, cloth-covered neck beneath the happy idiot face. My lips shaped the words they could not pronounce. "If you don't give me back my voice, I'll . . . "

"Cut it, the kid."

My little brother was standing next to the bed, his pale legs like sticks under his long, white nightshirt. His eyes were like saucers.

"It's all a matter of control," the grating, familiar voice whispered to me. "Now, take your hands off my throat and put them inside my chest, and everything will be fine. Remember, pally, I'll let you hold the strings, but it's your neck that's in the noose."

Distrustful, resentful, I had no choice but to comply.

"Who's that?" my brother asked.

"Me, I'm Mr. Nobody. Go back to sleep." My guest's mouth opened and shut in perfect synchronism with his words, but rather than lulling they piqued my brother's curiosity.

"Tell me, please. Please tell me, or I'll tell Mommy."

"All right," he said; and before I could stop him, he went too far. "I'm your new brother."

At that moment I could have cut the chord. Maybe I should have, but my own voice would have died with his. Now I had to let them go on. My real brother leaned eagerly forward.

"Where'd you come from?"

"Here we will go," I thought, "on the riddling merry-go-round."

His eyes were glowing like crystal balls. "Where I come from children study bird calls. Blind men play the harmonica. Every door is open, and butterflies make music with their wings." He whistled, as if to himself, "Oh, I could tell you stories."

On cue, my brother jumped. "Please. Pretty pretty please!"

"We-l-ll, all right." He drew us into a tight circle. "Let me tell you of the dummy who sat on an egg."

I was exhausted. I didn't want to hear this. I wanted to go to sleep. Maybe I would wake up alone. "Dream on," he said, then began.

"Once upon a time there was a dummy. A real blockhead. Now one day this dummy was strolling along, singing a song, when what should he see in the middle of the road but an enormous egg. It was maybe the size of this sleepy head here," he tapped me and I could have sworn I heard a knock. "Anyway, suddenly the egg said, 'Please, I want to see the world. Help me to hatch.' So the dummy climbed on top of the egg, and he sat there ... "

Dream I did—that I was in a universe of monkey-faced puppets. They went about their daily business, but I couldn't move my arms, because I had no strings. I couldn't move my legs without rods or crossbars, my head without a coil. I could see, I could sense, but lacking the proper mechanisms, I was immobile.

"After a while one of the dummy's friends came along and said, 'What are you doing, sitting on an egg in the middle of the road?'

"'I am helping it to hatch,' the dummy answered.

"'That's silly,' his friend told him. 'In order to hatch an egg you need heat. You should start a fire.'

"'Thank you for the advice,' said the dummy, and began to collect fallen tree limbs and flints."

The strings of all the monkey-faced puppets were attached to a gigantic hand in the clouds. I wanted to call to the hand to throw me a line. In the country of slaves the free man is a beggar. But I had no voice.

"Then the dummy's second friend came along and said, 'What are you doing, setting fire to an egg in the middle of the road?'

"'I am helping it to hatch,' the dummy answered.

"'That's silly,' his second friend told him. 'In order to hatch an egg you need motion. You should build a cradle.'

"'Thank you for the advice,' said the dummy, and began to collect reeds for a basket and twine."

The gigantic hand dipped and the monkey-faced puppets danced accordingly. The hand was wrinkled and wore a smooth silver ring on its index finger. The clouds were painted on cardboard. There was an audience, barely distinguishable beyond the sunny glare of the stage lights.

"Then a wise man came and said, 'What are you doing, blocking the road with this blazing, shaking egg?'

"'I am helping it to hatch,' the dummy answered.

I was trapped in a performance I couldn't escape. The only choice I had was between awareness and detachment. By ignoring the monkey-faced puppets, the painted clouds, and the gigantic hand I would best them. The audience might not be able to tell the difference, but inside, where it counted, I went to sleep.

I woke to hear the unwanted guest finishing his story to my avid young brother.

"Dummy, it takes a chicken to hatch an egg!"

If this had a secret meaning, like the parables of the sages, I was not clever enough to grasp it. Neither was I free enough to ignore it. The innocent tale, I knew in my heart, was wicked. I felt a consuming suspicion of its author. No matter whether his words hurt my neighbors or charmed my brother, they had the same incensing effect on me.

"If thine right hand offend thee, kiddo."

The phrase caught in the folds of my outer ear like a bottle at the edge of a maelstrom. There was a rushing, and then there was quiet. My brother was asleep. My parents were asleep. My guest and myself were the only two sentient beings in Proszowice. Wondering if he would ever leave, I began to make elaborate, lethal plans for his removal. There were such things as nets and chains.

"What do you think I am, a grizzly bear?"

As long as he could read my mind surprise was impossible. Then again, confrontation was inevitable. It occurred to me that I did not need to make myself audible to speak to him. I thought, "Thief!"

"He who is jealous, it is as if he were a thief."

"Jealous of what, of what is rightfully mine, my home, my family, my voice?"

"Thou shalt not covet."

"Me? I do not . . ."

"Like hell you don't. You not only covet my meager accomplishments but the possessions of others. Oh, not their material wealth, but their truest, most valuable goods, their talents and spirits. You covet the music of Hemtobble and the women of your friend Isaac. You covet the words of God as they pass through to the Kohanim. You covet the love of your parents for your siblings, and never consider the love they bear you. Why, you even covet your own voice. You are a monster of greed."

He shook me with his knowledge of my sins of pride and desire. I could not argue, but I would not tolerate this attack from a piece of verbose timber, hardly a saint. I did not need to be scourged; I needed to be cured, and for that I had to have the one tool of self-discovery and change: I needed my voice.

But was the music I envied any less evident in the arrangement of the notes? And was the virility of Isaac not on the page, the sanctity of the Kohanim not in their prayers? What did virtually all of the incidents my antagonist recalled, as well as his very recollection, prove if not that, although I might have lost my voice, I still had my words.

I sat up in bed and reached across the floor to the dresser. Its four drawers were filled with clothes, but the top surface was my private treasure store. On it were empty spools and strings and pictures I had cut out of magazines and interesting rocks I had found and a green leather notebook I had been given for my birthday. There was a candle stub in a tin plate and three red-tipped matches, one of which I pulled along the leg of my bed, drawing a flame out of the air, taming it with the misshapen piece of wax.

In the dim, flickering light I took my good pen, the one with the blue-black marbling, and dipped it into my inkwell. The sound was like a parched man's first draft. I leaned back, propped the notebook against my upraised knees, and let the slaked pen hover delicately over the surface of the paper. Now, I thought, what was this process I was embarking on? It was to transfer the voice inside me to the outside. I began to write:

"VENTRILOQUISM"

At the first touch of pen to paper my undesirable sleepover guest perked up. He was distinctly nervous. His eyes rolled in his head. He hummed to distract me, but it didn't work.

"Sometimes," I wrote, "*my thoughts were like fish. Evasive, obscure, deep. But when they rose to the surface I could reach into the pool of my self and spear them. The trident flashed, plunged. There was barely a ripple as it sliced the water. Threads of blood curled upward. The fish bucked furiously, but it was caught.*"

"Hey, watcha doing?"

Still speechless, I took a positive pleasure in my inability to answer. There was no hiding my purpose, though. Nor did I wish to give him the satisfaction of illicit discovery. I would allow, even encourage, him to peek as I reclaimed my voice on paper. He lunged for the notebook, but his body was undeveloped and easily blocked by my slight, human shoulder. "Not so fast!" I thought.

"Don't you know that's sacrilegious? Remember that a man's body is the temple of the Lord. Thou shalt not create graven images."

But I could swap Bible with the best of them. "Be fruitful and multiply," I thought. "That applies to fish, people, and words. Any new voice strengthens the chorus of praise to the One and Only. To add to life is to increase the celestial gift, to hasten the dawn of the Messiah."

"No, no, listen, you don't know what you're doing. You're tampering with forces beyond your control." I could sense a hint of his fear that I might be able to throw off his yoke and regain my dominion, in which case woe be to him. *"I could extract them, examine them, peel off the scales, remove the bones, devour the meat."*

"Enough!"

"Still, the essence of the creature was withheld from me."

In frustration he tried to blow out the candle. I heard the "whssh" and reached over to protect the vulnerable light, but it wavered more from my motion than from his breath. I heard another, louder "whssh," then another, and another, until the dim attic room seemed to contain a tornado, but the slender flame burned on with steadfast grace.

I waited, my pen poised menacingly.

"All right," he surrendered. "It's all a matter of control. Now, shut your mouth. . . . Now, from the stomach, speak to me. . . . I said, shut your mouth if you ever want to talk again. Now, let's hear it, you dummy."

"Rrr. Ehh," was all the sound I could muster.

"That's right. You see, it's not so easy. Now just imagine that your mouth is made out of wood; hey, a little sympathy please."

"Nbll."

He whispered directions to me. "It's a matter of control. Tense those stomach muscles, breathe deeply. Now, between your chest and abdomen, under your heart, can you feel a kind of ridge? that's your diaphragm. You make that go, the rest will be natural. Now c'mon, pally, you're so big on the Bible, repeat after me, 'In the beginning.'"

"Nstbegista."

"There was the Word."

"Nrstaworsta."

"Keep your mouth shut, pull your tongue back, and wiggle the tip. Keep the diaphragm taut. Vibrate."

Sounds somewhere between creaks and groans came from me. It felt as if my throat were petrified, as if the voice struggling to emerge was something physical lodged there, maybe a snake.

"C'mon, contract those lungs . . . exhale. In. Out. In. Out. Exhale, and the sound is . . . there!"

It burst from me, a high, hoarse yelp that faded into a soft, satisfied, "whssh."

"That's better. Now you've only got to learn what to say."

I was invulnerable to his wisecracks. In the one moment of release my original strength doubled. Reassured by my new voice on paper, the voice I was born with reassured its literary twin in turn. You scratch my vowels, I'll scratch yours. In fact, with the return of my ability to speak at will, I wished only to write more. I lowered the raised pen and continued: "*It was a quiet day, not long after my first expeditions into the outside world had come to their various, dismal ends.*"

"Hey! I thought we agreed. None of that."

"I'm just recounting my day."

"*My* day, baby, *mine;* and every word of it diminishes me. You're stealing my life."

"You should talk. You stole my voice."

"I *am* your voice, idiot. Put me on paper—I die."

"I'm sorry," I said. (I really was.) "But you forced me to do this. I don't think I can listen.

"Don't think then."

"*I had retreated from the zone of the imagination. . . .* "

"Retreat, retreat," he pleaded. "Otherwise I . . . I disappear." Indeed, his face seemed a shade paler.

"*I played; I prayed; I ate my mother's chulent.*"

"Do that! Do that! Why can't you be content like anyone else?"

" *. . . sometimes in patterns like pentacles or Jewish stars.*"

"Don't you know when to stop?"

"*I trod my worries into the fertile Polish earth.*"

His body, through which I thought I could see the window sash, began to rise.

"*It was not the specifically thoughtful nature of these walks but the random thoughts they engendered, like fish . . .* "

He was hovering two feet over the bed, like a cloud.

"*I was beside the river, under my favorite tree, when a voice hailed me.*"

"Well, boy," he said. "This is where I came in. See you between the lines." And up he floated, graceful as a fish in water, toward the window. His body was drawn like smoke through the crack, which sealed after him.

I leapt out of bed, placed my hands on the virgin glass, and gazed up into the brooding sky. I could see nothing, but I could swear that I heard him say, "Hey, pally, I think I can do it!"

The BLUE-Eyed
Jew

oses descended from heaven to listen to Rabbi Akiva. The great prophet personally received the Torah on Mount Sinai, still he came to heed the words of another. So if widsom did not stop with Moses, why should wisdom stop with the rabbis? Tell me why we can't examine the Bible in the light of modern learning?" The speaker was Jacob Lester, in front of the shul. Maybe he was too superstitious to say these things inside the shul.

"There was an age for prophecy. There was an age for interpretation. Now is an age for obedience," the Rabbi said.

"Now is the age for electricity," Jacob replied, although there was none for fifty miles.

"Since when doesn't a candle give light?"

"In America, every house has electricity—and running water. In America . . ."

"Enough!" The Rabbi was angry. "If you are so enamored for America, then perhaps you should go there."

"Perhaps I shall."

The argument was repeated a thousand times, in a thousand different ways. In opposition to the rabbinical establishment, Jacob Lester was our enlightenment. He cut his hair and wore a blue satin waistcoat that glimmered under his gabardine. It matched his eyes— a shocking, gentile sky color.

It was said that when Lester was young he had been a brilliant scholar. Pondering the Law one day, he fell into the village well and cracked his skull and was never the same. Both physically and intellectually, his head changed shape. The broken bones set into a high-domed, simian cast, as he made his first evolutionist remarks.

Someone answered him, "You may come from the monkeys, but we don't."

He began to comb his hair in a futile attempt to disguise his deformity, and before you knew it he was the barber's best customer. Like Samson, that first snip of the scissors ruined him. He cut his sidelocks and beard; his swollen face was as clean as a woman's.

Vanity led to heresy.

"You watch out for him," Reb Tellman told our class. "You see what happens when you fail to study the Torah."

Of course, my teacher's warnings only served to intrigue me. I listened to Jacob's tales of America with a fascination my peers reserved for Sodom and Gomorrah. I followed his every flamboyance with my own Semitic walnut eyes. In shul, he flipped the pages of the prayer book as if cross-checking the facts. I half expected him to leap from his seat crying, "Aha! a contradiction!" He was always broadcasting the latest news of the world for the elders to shake their heads over. "In America," he said, "they dance naked."

In Proszowice, the women wore ragged dresses topped with old shirts covered by raveling sweaters and, usually, a shawl. While their husbands studied, they did the work of the oxen they resembled. They washed and mopped with the two heavy buckets of water they carried from the well each day. This daily subservience to the well was Lester's particular bugbear.

"You see," he raved, "in America they have indoor plumbing, therefore more hygiene, therefore better health, therefore a longer life to study the Torah. Hence plumbing is holy."

They laughed at him, and Jacob retreated into sullen quiet.

I sympathized with any outsider, but my own problems were too great for me to join his cause. If the Rabbi represented the past and Jacob Lester the future, where was the present? Oh, I had my moments, limited intuitions of something wonderful just out of reach.

After a night of visions of a kingdom of plenty at the base of a golden throne, its crown lost in the clouds over my headboard, I was reluctant to wake. My bed was five inches too high to step directly down from, and I was afraid that the small jolt would burst the night's iridescent bubble; I decided that those five inches were all that separated me from accomplishing my goals. I slid back under the quilt.

"I'm warning you," my mother said, "if you don't get up and go to school this minute, I'll call your father."

I smiled, because my father was as likely to say, "I don't blame you, sometimes life is tough," and crawl in beside me as he was to explain the necessity for responsibility. Nevertheless, I rose.

Because I had dawdled, breakfast was hurried. I was in a fretful mood and sought omens of ill favor. From the broken dream through the cold oatmeal, I created images of my discontent in the world about me.

The town square was a lumpy table with sheds and carts like misshapen pottery scattered around its edges. I knew all the merchants, and they called out to me.

"Your brother's been by an hour ago."

"Your father's looking for you."

One fruit vendor threw me a peach that had a large purple bruise. "These ladies," he said, "they come, put their fingers through the skin, ruin the produce. Why? To see if there are pits for all I know. I can't sell this. If you're hungry, then eat!"

Our deal was tacit. I listened to him, then I got a reward. The peach was delicious, but the town too small. If I were five inches taller I could earn my own keep and buy peaches without bruises. In the meantime, what sort of figure did I cut among the townfolk? Maybe that of a small gray mouse terrified of its own shadow but too stupid to recognize cats.

I was approaching the cheder when a soccer ball escaped one of my classmates. The rough leathery sphere flew at me. I loped forward to return it with a side kick, but it bounced awkwardly off a pebble and I lunged too far. I heard the muscle in my thigh tear like a piece of waxed paper. The next thing I knew I was on the ground in pain while the stupid ball rolled to a halt several meters away. I felt that my miss was a moral failure.

I did not want to go to school. Reb Tellman would hurt me: for being late, for not doing my homework, for being the distracted, dissatisfied boy I was. Such punishment had occurred before in retribution for a multitude of academic sins; I was familiar with the sting of the rod. It probably bothered me less than the effort to make the blows worthwhile did my teacher, but I would have preferred to avoid the evil balance. I glanced at the sky.

"Instead of looking up, the trick is to look down." The speaker was Jacob Lester. "The rabbis have their heads in the clouds, so they trip over their own feet. If they were truly interested in divinity, they would adopt the God's-eye view. Examine the earth from which we descend. Descend."

I didn't entirely comprehend this theory. I thought it was Darwin's. That was a name I recognized, latest in a genealogy of troublemakers from Jonah through Spinoza, a name to entice and repel. I knew no limits, but still!—Darwin!

"I know what you're thinking."

"Yes?"

"Yes. You wish you had a napkin to wipe that stuff off your chin before a bee comes to bite it off."

I stroked my chin. "That's not true. There's no juice here."

"Who said I was talking about juice? I was referring to that bit of beard you have. Maybe you're wishing that your little locks didn't get tangled so often."

The "beard" he mentioned was one single hair that sprouted from a mole on my neck. I was very sensitive about this and reached up to shield it.

"Yes, you've got quite a little growth there. It's high time you took account of your maturity, young man. As a matter of fact, I was just going to get my hair cut. Would you like to accompany me?"

Despite the mockery in Lester's voice, there was something flattering about the thought of my adulthood. I also enjoyed the idea of a shave. "No," I said. "I have to go to school."

The barbershop was all white tile and mirrors. It smelled of lotions and tonics and porcelain cups full of congealed lather and leather strops. Two large tear-shaped bottles filled with red liquid flanked two chairs, one of which was occupied by a man who resembled a mummy because his face was wrapped in steaming white towels. Jergenchic, the barber, peered at me suspiciously.

"Don't worry," Lester said, "we're going to the well," as if that should answer any questions.

Jergenchic gave a professional shrug.

"Yes, sir," said Jacob, sweeping into the open seat as if it were a throne, "that's another difference between rabbis and scientists. The latter study animals; the former look like them. Don't forget the sideburns. In America, they take baths every day, twice on Shabbos."

I sat on the bench, silently absorbing his blasphemy. I agreed but could no more respect him than the community did. The only thing Jacob could have done to prove his seriousness was to emigrate, but in America there was no shortage of Americans and, blue eyes notwithstanding, he would be just another Jew.

The man/mummy slept.

Afterward, Jacob took me to the well.

The well had been dug by the first Jews to come to Poland from Spain. There was still a rusted metal ornament on it that bore traces of the Mediterranean. The water was a distant inky mirror that made me pensive.

"The origin," Jacob Lester pronounced.

This echoed my reflections, but I didn't want to admit it. I thought of the young Jacob, balancing obscure philosophical details, tumbling. Like the forefather whose name he bore, Jacob had worked years to achieve repose, only to be betrayed at the well. Still, he set to work again. This was admirable, but I couldn't wait. Five inches separated me from my goal, and I aimed to bridge them. "How deep is it?"

He shook his head. "I never measured. But you know..." he rested his arms on the rim of the well as he gazed down into it, a gypsy searching a crystal ball for his destiny, "In America..."

I had heard enough about the land of opportunity. I thought of the ocean one had to cross in order to get there. It was larger than Europe. The ships that crossed it were larger than Proszowice. They had electricity and . . . "Running water," I muttered.

"Yes," Jacob replied.

"What about walking on it?"

"Today we can all work miracles, thanks to modern technology."

I noted the water bucket, hooked onto a spit. It occurred to me that if inspiration followed the dredging of dye into a fountain pen there must be worlds of intelligence and vitality here. We could all work miracles—despite modern technology. Pipes and pumps, who needed them? The thing was to examine the unrevealed force that generates. I bent over the gaping hole, then lifted one leg with the care of a stork and stepped into the hanging bucket.

"What are you doing?" Jacob's eyes glittered with alarm.

The bucket felt as if it were a balloon. It swayed back and forth and bumped lightly against the mossy wall. I rummaged through my pockets: lint, a sourball, scraps of paper with notes to myself, an interesting rock, the head of a toy soldier, a zloty. That was what I was looking for. It seemed an eternity falling, and then there was a tiny, sad "plunk."

I said, "Make a wish."

"I wish you would get out of there and go to school."

"In America, they study nature."

"In Proszowice, they study Torah."

Suspended, I felt anchored, and the world seemed flimsy. Direction, dimension, character, and history had no meaning. Here the apostle of progress was calling on tradition to ground me. Here was a man of the world terrified by the whim of a dark-eyed child. I made a joke, gleaned from the idle musings of my afternoon. "I just wanted to see what the American wants to see."

But Jacob rose to the unintentional lure. "What?"

So I continued. "That man, the one in the barbershop, the one under the towels, he's an American."

"Don't make fun."

"I thought it was arranged by you. I thought that was who you were talking to."

"I don't know why you persist."

The trick to lying well is never to press your point. Let the gull back you off and leave it to him to take the bait. Jacob said, "Why should an American come here?"

He had forgotten that I was sitting in a bucket over a well and that my statement was likely to be as ludicrous as my position. "Down there," I gestured languidly beneath me, improvising. "The old foundation stones, they have inscriptions. Ancient writings of primitive peoples." I was at an advantage because Jacob himself was a user of spurious logic and thus bound to be susceptible to the same. "He's a researcher. He wants to get an exhibit together, to tour New York. He has blue eyes, like you."

"No-o-o." His soft, impressed denial meant, "No kidding!"

"Maybe I'm wrong." And that convinced him. Once a liar acknowledges the unreality of his story, the extraordinary becomes mundane and therefore palatable. Find something that someone wants to believe, and he will find a way to believe it.

"Maybe I should talk to him. I mean, I have experience. New York." Jacob's voice was as eager as an adolescent's, and suddenly, I felt ashamed. I could hardly admit that the "American" I had conjured up was probably a sleeping tailor.

"Wait. . . ." I did not want to witness Jacob's disappointment. I did not want to see his eyes dim. "Lower me," I commanded, like a general ordering his troops to cover his flight. I didn't know how I had become so imperious, but there was something about having shaped another person's world that gave one legitimate power over him.

Jacob was nervous. He circled the well, reknotted his tie, hoping, I supposed, that I would change my mind.

But I was adamant. If he had fallen twenty years ago, he could not refuse to grant someone else that risk. He coiled the loose rope around his shoulder, braced one foot on the dusty cornerstone, and unlatched the bucket. He sagged with the burden and the mechanism groaned. The slow cranking began. My ship disembarked, but as soon as my head sank below the top rim, out of sight of land, it halted. A tremulous voice enquired, "Enough?"

"Keep going."

"I don't like this."

"Descend."

His eyes were the sky, clouding over with grief. "You don't know what you're doing, what you're making me do," he complained as he continued to unwind the rope to lower me step by jolting step. "You don't know what's down there. Once Mrs. Horowitz brought up a fish. Gills in her dishwater. She fainted." It sounded as though he might faint, not from effort but from fear. I heard him, as if remembering, say, "It's terrible."

Now a stray carp did not seem so terrible to me, but I did begin to have my doubts. As the light from the sun grew indirect and the walls began to close in, I wondered if there were monsters as well as fish at the bottom of the well. Who knew where the dark waters seeped in from, what underground passages they led to, what worlds they touched? I was on the verge of reversing directions when Jacob called out, "I don't care. I'm pulling you out."

That was the wrong thing for him to say. I took the penknife I used to sharpen pencils out of my pocket. Its blade shone like a crescent moon in the night. At first touch, two strands frayed off the braided chain, and two by two the threads separated as my steel bit deeper.

Lester yelled, "No!" and frantically jerked me upward. I sawed as furiously as he cranked, when suddenly I heard an awful, strangled cry and something like an enormous bat swooped out of the shadows. It was Jacob.

I didn't know if he had leapt, slipped, had been pushed or pulled by the weight of the bucket, but once he fell, I followed. My hand was burned by the friction of the sliding rope. Then came a splash, a shock. The water sucked me under. Jacob and I flailed desperately against the undertow. There were caverns and currents that drew us along locomotively. I felt like a fish, but I could not swim.

It wasn't life that flashed before me but a series of discrete images: water and the flaming rope, then the column of smoke seen in the Sinai four thousand years before. There were pictures of dummies and violins and bicycles, a taste of lox, the scent of perfumed letters and earthen tombs, a premonition of greenhouses.

Then I came to the surface, gasping air like a man in the desert gulps water, coughing water like phlegm. I clawed onto the bobbing wooden bucket. It was a raft adrift, riding the waves created by my fall. I dragged Jacob on board. We could have been in the North Atlantic, the sole survivors of an unconsummated passage to America. My legs wiggled beneath the surface like a jellyfish's tentacles. We waited for the storm to clear in order to survey the dimensions of our loss. My ankles, knees, and thighs were immersed. My belly was cushioned by the bucket. I touched bottom; the water was chest high.

Neither Jacob nor I wondered aloud how the water could have seemed so deep yet been so shallow. The Proszowice sky was a blue eye in the darkness, a distant star to chart us home. We both stood, but still kept a hand on the floating bucket for the illusion of safety.

Until my sight had adjusted to the darkness, I examined my surroundings by touch. I felt the rough-hewn stones and the moss, and a large, hard-backed insect that scurried away from my inquisitive fingers. A stretch of the cut rope sat on the water like a dead snake. I smelled vegetation. I began to discern the gray-green colors and the chalky lines from past floods like age rings on a tree. One was five inches above my head.

"There," I pointd to the ghostly ribbon. It looked like a line of ancient text, but since it was in a circle there was no way to determine where it started and where it ended. "There too." I pointed to the defacements of time and insisted that they were the signatures of an extinct people, carved millennia ago so that we could witness their existence. "Do you think they were Jewish?"

Jacob said nothing. He was sunken within himself—perhaps in recollection of twenty years back or anticipation of twenty years ahead, perhaps in the betrayal of his past or the present betrayal or some betrayal yet to come. I could see his unblinking blue eyes.

"Hey!" I shook him.

"In America . . ." he said, and for a second I was relieved to hear his usual refrain. But he continued in a strange, volitionless monotone, the voice of a torture victim confessing to a crime he did not commit. "The ten tribes live there. Someone should help them. Someone should tell them to return to the paths of their ancestors."

The brash, enlightened skin had peeled off to reveal the troubled inner shadow. I was embarrassed. "You know what?" I said. "If all these lost people could make their marks here, why can't we? Here, I'll show you how." Still clutching the penknife in my unburnt hand, I set to carve my initials on the wall.

With the first scratch, Jacob awoke from his trance and began to scream. "Help! Someone please help me. HEL-L-LP!"

I reached out to calm him, but he recoiled as if my fingers were a branding iron. "It's not so bad," I said, and I believed it. Actually, I was beginning to feel rather at home. The water was cool, the light a mild refraction from above. I felt a real communion with the people I had imagined writing their names, and I looked forward to someone reading mine in the future. Jacob's shrieks, however, grew worse with every soothing gesture I made. As I tried to placate him, I therefore sought to escape him. I put my heart and muscle into the knife and chipped away at the second of my three initials.

My every talent was concentrated on the tip of the knife, digging sense out of the brutal rock face. As the letter emerged, though, that sense did communicate itself to Jacob, and his cries became words. He was miserable, and in his misery turned vicious. "So who will read this? How many years will it take? Do you think they'll be Jewish? And what of their eyes?"

And I understood him. Jacob Lester's obsession with the new world, it dawned on me, was a mask for his devotion to the old. He had the kind of character that needed a geography for his thoughts, but if here, in Proszowice, he said, "in Proszowice," he would be a moron. Instead he said, "in America," which might as well have been "in Bolivia" or "in Mongolia." Under the strain of his pose he might actually leave Poland someday, simply to be able to refer backward with ease. Wherever he went, Jacob would bring his community with him; wherever I went, I brought exile.

The first to come rushing to rescue us was the man who was the mummy in the barbershop. I recognized his collar and the cut of his hair. I also recognized his face and the Semitic walnut eyes that were a mirror to mine. How, from some five or ten meters down in a vertical tunnel, could I see him? How could I fail? He was my father.

A circle formed. They devised a plan to free Jacob and me from our captivity. As they were doing so, I reached up, five inches over my head, and carved my first message to the world, my first poem, into the stone at the bottom of the well. "In Proszowice," I wrote, "is America."

And the good people descended.

New Words

for Old

t sometimes happens that a man reading the Torah cannot make out one of the letters within the holy scripture. The fabric is old, the ink faded. Although the sacred documents have been read over and over again from time out of time, although they are known backwards and forwards, in the blood, they are never merely recited and the reader cannot presume upon his memory. We Jews have a great respect for the written word, so that as it is written it must be read. In the year that passes between one reading of a portion and the next, the words may be miraculously changed by the Holy One, blessed be He. If a word cannot be discerned, if there is the slightest doubt, an expert is called upon to resolve the dilemma. That expert's decision is final. That expert is a child.

The theory is that a child's eyesight is keener than an adult's. He is not asked for a theological interpretation. he is simply asked whether the third letter in the seventh word on the first line of the page is a *vov* or a *yud*.

Following the same logic, when the famous poet Kimminov came to our town, a child was chosen to put his youthful ear close to the ancient mouth and repeat its hushed words of poetic wisdom. Unfortunately, none of those involved in effecting this piece of Talmudic reasoning realized that between the ear and the mouth the words would have to pass through the brain of the child—and therein lies this story.

My body was at school, my mind far from it. In this dream there was no dark wood desk enclosing me like a medieval torture device. There were no smells of chalk and moldy textbooks. There was no Proszowice, period. I was sick of my home and the twelve years I had spent there. I was in Cracow, in a fine apartment above a nightclub, and a great gas fire was blazing on the hearth. I had a neatly trimmed beard that would make my father faint, and twirling her red-painted fingernails in my goatee was a girl who would make my mother faint. I was a fabulously successful young author and she was my protégé.

I was offering her a glass of champagne. A silver bucket with chipped ice glittering like diamonds sat beneath me as I unwrapped the foil and inched the cork up out of the bottle. It was about to pop. I could feel the tension . . . when, out of the blue, SLAP, down on my fingers, came the length of the ruler.

I leapt from my seat with a cry of pain and outrage.

SLAP and SLAP again, until the pain overwhelmed the fury and I was completely submissive. I felt as if my entire arm had been plunged into a vat of tanner's acid.

SLAP once more for good measure, and I was a sobbing, wailing ruin.

Reb Tellman stood glowering over me, his lips compressed within his bristly red beard, his eyes tiny concentrated beads of bitter fire, and the ruler raised like an ax. It was a stance familiar to me, for since my earliest years I had been susceptible to the giving of offense, but whenever my father or my old melamed, Reb Chaim Ludsky, beat me I could see that they suffered as much as I did. Even as their switches cut the air they seemed to cry, "Why do you make me do this?" Also, they seldom used their full strength and their switchings seldom hurt. Reb Tellman, however, hurt. Reb Tellman enjoyed his task.

Like myself, Reb Tellman was a dreamer, like myself, the worst kind of dreamer, a poet. I had sensed a bond with him when the other students made fun of me and my verse, calling me "the Jewish jingler," their idea of wit. The usually taciturn melamed descended like a bird of prey, and my tormentors scattered before him, but when I tried to thank him he fixed me with a baleful stare and hissed, "They're right!"

Less than a month later, Reb Tellman took us on a nature hike. We packed challah, hard-boiled eggs, and jugs of water and ate them amid a copse of birch trees. Reb Tellman, who had been anxious and distracted all morning, took a sheaf of paper from a bag he had been clutching. It was poetry he read to us—terrible, sentimental poetry about the Palestinian homeland of the Jews. Others had written on the subject, but instead of their sweet, anticipatory vision there emerged a pathetic, impotent hatred of life as lived by the poet. The reading was followed by an embarrassing silence. The thin, speckled trunks of the birches waved in the breeze. Reb Tellman's pallid face turned rusty, and he said, "Enough of this. We must return." He never told us the author's name.

"I will ask you one more time," he said, silhouetted against the cheder's single window like a statue. "What does Rabbi Eliezer have to say of the role of the poets in the time of the Messiah?"

He always asked me questions the answers to which I would hate. I sniffed back my tears and looked him in the eye. "He says there shall be no need for them, nor for any artist, because everything shall be perfect." Actually, I thought that everyone then would be a poet or an artist, with the possible exception of Reb Tellman, and that would be why everything was perfect. Adversity makes for certainty in a particularly stubborn type of soul. But whereas I openly avowed my poetic intent, Reb Tellman considered his something shameful. That, I think, is why he hated me and beat me: envy.

Obviously, not everyone in Proszowice could appreciate the muse as my evil genius and I. To most, poetry was an aberration, inspired by lazy, no-good gadabouts with self-proclaimed emancipated tendencies. Strangely, they did appreciate Kimminov. He was a half-breed partaking of both idol and pariah, a religious man, a literary man. Jewish successes in the non-Jewish world were few, and therefore to be treasured. Not emulated, but treasured enough so that when he was to pass through our little town on his way to receive the honor due him in the big city, it was a big deal. A public holiday was declared to wish him good speed. The people could feel their blood race with pride in their landsman's accomplishments, and then let that blood subside into its usual, godly torpor.

Having impressed the fact of the uselessness of poets on the class's mind and my knuckles, Reb Tellman led us out into the square to welcome one. We were a flock of baby penguins, identical in our short black pants, our white shirts with the tsitsis fringes hanging down. Oblivious to this ignoble situation, the other boys played, glad for the recess. I could not keep my eyes from the road. I craned forward to be closer to the great man, wherever beyond the bend he was. In front of our store, I could see my father. Sensing my eyes upon him, that marvelous, intuitive man turned. He could have been a poet. He knew of my inner turmoil, for he had seen me propped up in bed, chewing meditatively on my favorite fountain pen, thinking and writing by the light of the crescent moon. He did not understand this; but he was understanding nonetheless, and I loved him for that.

Then I saw it.

The subdued earth colors of the carriage were the same as the road, and for a moment I thought it was a mirage, and then it was upon us. There was a rattling, which I felt in my bones— and it was beyond us.

"So what?" Moshele Rosen said, but I did not deign to answer. I had caught only a flash of the reflective gray window, but I felt a thrilling communion with the ghostly visage behind it. Had there been the single illuminating glint I thought flew from the insubstantial profile like a sunbeam through the trees into my heart, or had I imagined it? No matter. As they passed, I yearned to throw myself under the wheels, to be carried away wherever their master might go, away.

I glanced briefly at Reb Tellman in childish triumph, but he too was caught in the moment, looking after the carriage, his eyes tearing from the cloud of dust it raised.

There was commotion in front of the shul. People were running into the street. A lightning bolt, no less! The carriage had stopped.

One of the horses had slipped a brace. For the last two hours they had been riding on edge, praying to reach Proszowice before the creature broke loose and left them stranded. The horse, bearing an expression of patient suffering on its long face, was bleeding along a thin line across its back where the uneven harness had rubbed. The animal would have to be replaced and, of course, the brace would have to be repaired, all of which would take several hours, so that instead of a quick glimpse, we had the unexpected honor of the actual presence of the great man.

Pleskin, the innkeeper, came elbowing through the crowd and offered a tall glass on a silver platter up to the gray window. "An iced tea, sir? You must be parched."

I was jumping up and down, frantic to see through the mass of Proszowicer that surrounded me. Then, from nowhere, a benign arm lifted me above the sea of covered heads. I was weightless and about to pat my father's strong shoulder for pleasure when a wrinkled hand like a bird's claw came into view through the carriage window, and my heart stopped. What words had that hand crafted? Though shriveled and gruesome as a Christian relic, these were noble fingers that no man alive would dare to hit with a ruler, that my own unlined extremities ached to become.

There was a hurried consultation between the Rabbi and a few village elders. A unique opportunity had presented itself to them and they didn't quite know how to respond. They had to balance their inherent distrust of poetry against their pride in the poet and their awareness of the honor it would be for our village to host such a man. Aesthetics played no part whatsoever in their decision, but they made the aesthetic choice. God alone, blessed be He, knows why Kimminov accepted.

"Our home is your home," the Rabbi greeted him. "Despite the unfortunate circumstances of your arrival, we welcome you and hope your stay will be as happy as it is brief. You may even show us a sample of your work? You may read for us?"

There was a hush while we waited in a semicircle around the carriage window, which even from my literally exalted position my vision still could not penetrate. If the answer was no it would be an insult to the entire community, if yes, an unprecedented acknowledgment. There was no in-between.

There was an in-between. The silence was broken by the faintest rumble imaginable. If not the words, the meaning, however, was clear. Kimminov would read if he could, but he couldn't: he had no voice. There were rumors of the demon yells of his youth, but in his declining years he was practically mute.

"Perhaps you have something written down that our cantor could read for you?" the Rabbi asked.

"Why," Kimminov whispered hoarsely, "should I carry the printed copy when I have the original here?" and he apparently tapped his ancient temple.

That was when someone had the bright idea of Kimminov whispering his verses line by line and someone repeating them.

Who should have this signal honor?

The Rabbi? But he was a little hard of hearing himself. He would be glad to introduce the reading. The cantor? But he was tall, and it would be undignified for him to have to stoop. He would be glad to offer a benediction.

Across the way I saw a gleam in my teacher Reb Tellman's eye. He suggested that it should "perhaps be someone with a poetic gift himself" and he cast his eyes downward, not with modesty, but in the need to hide their lupine hunger.

Kimminov rasped, "It will take more than the poetic gift to hear me. More of an auditory gift, I think."

I think he was trying to evade the ordeal as gracefully as possible. It might have worked had not my splendid shopkeeper of a father not mused absentmindedly about what would happen if the Torah for some unforeseen reason could not be read, God forbid.

"Of course!" the Rabbi crowed, and drew the analogy with a smudged letter of Holy Writ. Of course Kimminov could not allow a solution good enough for the word of the Lord to dissatisfy him. A child would serve as the messenger of the human writ.

Taking into account the excellent earlier suggestion of one with a feeling for words, as well as the requisite youth, as well as one who, literally head and shoulders above the rest, happened to be in clear sight of the assembled multitude, the messenger was chosen. Need you guess who?

The shul was as crowded as if it were Yom Kippur, and though the Torahs had been removed from the ark in order to secularize the only building large enough to contain the throng, a religious air still clung to the planks of the floor and the rafters. Of course, now there was elation instead of lament. The day of judgment had come and gone; this was a day of reward. Kimminov would compensate for every symphony orchestra and every opera that had bypassed us on its tour of the great cities. It was the biggest event since the wedding of Isaac the Millionaire. All were dressed in their ragged finest, the men having brushed their beards for the occasion, the women with large red circles for lips. It was our own queer parody of a first night, the aimless milling and eager chattering increasing as more and more people made their appearance. There should have been a doorman to bow and scrape and announce their names. "Hear ye! Hear ye! Zalman the Digger and his lovely shrew. Hear ye! Hear ye! Mrs. Horowitz and her three unmarried daughters. Hear ye! Hear ye!"

Reb Tellman was a literary lion, explaining the difference between epic and lyric. Another group delved into the intricacies of rhyme and meter, while a third cluster discussed money. My father and mother entered with a quiet pride, but despite themselves became the center of yet another whirlpool of activity. By far the largest of these overlapping circles surrounded Kimminov. He was Proszowice's statement of worth to the world.

My feet were planted as a willow, my hands like its branches in a hurricane, shaking, twitching, rubbing my thighs and stroking my slicked-down hair and small velvet skullcap. In preparation for the words of wisdom they were to hear, my ears had been scoured as never before, a tiny rag squeezed in to tickle my brain. I had been scrubbed as briskly as a fancy woman's fingernails. I hummed up and down imaginary scales in order to better serve the poetry. I thought great thoughts and endeavored to make myself pure.

Simultaneously the Rabbi began his introduction, while one of the elders gave me last-minute instructions. I could comprehend neither, the "poet laureate of Eastern Judaism" getting mixed up with "listening like you would to the Kohanim." There was a buzzing as if a bee were caught in my ear, and my attention was glued to the figure walking across the platform toward me.

He reminded me of gentile mythical creatures—elves, imps, sprites; he was not much taller than myself but had a huge beard that flowed most of the way down his chest. His skin was covered with a mountain range of warts and birthmarks and liver-spots; his eyes were lakes of astonishing blue clarity. He was dressed like a beggar, his pants loose, his suit baggy, his hat a rumpled felt, out from under which his uncombed hair straggled to meet his beard. What was there within that strange apparition that made for poetry? I thought of Shakespeare with his goatee so pointed it could be used for a compass and ruffles up to his exquisitely powdered neck, exactly everything a writer should be, most especially in control, whereas Kimminov seemed the random victim of circumstance. But then I thought of myself and the ridiculous figure I must be cutting with my short pants and wide eyes, and decided that we were all brothers beneath the surface. I drew myself up to my full height, insignificant as it was, and tried to look straight back, to say with my stance, "I too am a poet."

But Kimminov was not asking any question that would merit such an answer. He was merely curious, looking at me the way I might look at something with eight legs. Then he smiled, clapped his gnarled hand on my back, and led me to the podium, where the Rabbi had just finished speaking. The audience was already on its feet, cheering its greeting, cheering him for being there, and themselves, and me.

Absolutely impassive, the old man stood until the cheers subsided, calmly surveying the people of my life as he had ten thousand crowds before, as he would ten thousand crowds again. I thought he could outstare the sun. I too was staring, but straight down onto the devotional blue cloth trimmed with silver thread that covered the podium. I played nervously with one of the fringes, and, ugly, awful as my poet was, I would have given anything in the world to change places with him.

And then it started. His voice was like a tea kettle at the point between bubbling and whistling. It was certainly as moist, as he spit into my ear. The words, a jumble at first, began to separate themselves, and, as per my instructions, I began to repeat them:

> Over the arctic ice.
> Over the frozen tundra.
> In the land of perpetual night.
> The Indians pray to a dark God.
> And wait for the light.

My voice cracked, then steadied. The words emerged from my mouth like the sound of a trumpet. I did not understand them, and neither, I think, did the congregation; but despite ourselves we felt something. In those few words, as rerecited by yours truly, Kimminov had created a world that swept over the moment like the shadow of a cloud. It was a miracle. Or a trick.

His breath was hot, its smell fetid, but I didn't mind. It was the salty sweet ocean breeze I felt, and its gentle tumble to shore I heard and did my best to repeat. I was a loudspeaking statue. They had such machines in Cracow. You whispered into one end and your voice boomed forth from the other. Well, maybe my pitch and cadence were different than Kimminov's, but my words were the same. I mean his words. I mean I felt truly inspired to be ministering to this palpable glory, but the green-eyed monster within me was awakening as I dared to glance up and saw my teacher in the front row.

Reb Tellman was squirming with discomfort. He was trying to listen to the poet without my benign intervention. He wanted to be where I was, and that made me squirm. I felt the first nibbling pangs of jealousy. I would willingly have abdicated my position to Reb Tellman, because there was another, more illustrious place I aspired to.

The ducts, tubes, tiny reverberating bones and membranes of my ear all worked properly, as did the parts of my mouth. My brain, however, could not help but work as well, and a giant hand within me wrapped itself around my heart and squeezed.

> And the day arose.
> Or so the Bible says.
> Eve in recumbent innocence.
> Adam the first.
> Adam the blessed . . .

the hoary, God-fearing poet thus began his version of the tale of the first temptation and fall, and I repeated it faithfully. There was such grace, such power, in his words that I wondered if there was a second set of commandments for poets that included "Thou shalt not covet thy neighbor's words."

> Thus spake the unbidden angel.
> The snake in his venom.
> The snake . . .

And something in me rebelled. Just as the moment in the unfolding legend was critical, so in the poem something was wrong. "The snake . . . the snake," echoed through me. Deliberate repetition I understood; it was for emphasis, resonance; but here it was from lack of imagination. I too was a writer, and I knew of such lapses, but I would not let a poem go until I had remedied them. I would sit and think and think until it hurt, until I found a word that seemed perfect and unique in all the world at that moment. Never would I have used the word *snake* twice in the same stanza. I would have preferred *viper* or *serpent,* or might have gone two exotic steps too far with *cobra, python,* or *anaconda.*

So I said:

> Thus spake the unbidden angel.
> The snake in his venom.
> The viper . . .

Silence. Shivering. I felt as if I had been bitten by a rattler, as if a poison were suddenly flooding up from the base of my spine, paralyzing me. At this point either time stopped or the poison spread, because nothing happened. No thunderbolt came out of the sky to split my head. No angry cry came from the audience to rip me to pieces. I looked up guiltily. They didn't know. It was that simple. That single word *viper* was mine, and by listening to it and accepting it, so was everyone in the shul. And they were none the worse for it. *Viper* was better than *snake*. It was different, and the *v* subliminally reinforced the word *venom* before it. It was just good poetry.

A fog of Kimminov's rancid breath enveloped my ear. I had forgotten him. Was he cursing me? No, he was quoting:

> The first man.
> With fists of gold.
> His loin girded.
> His life complete.

Poetry! He hadn't noticed. Of course not. Kimminov was old and feeble, no more alive than a rotting tree stump. He could whisper whatever he wanted, but how could he know what I repeated to the audience? My secret was safe with my viper.

But I was not safe from my viper. There was more, much more, that he could do for me, he whispered, hinting of the tree of knowledge. "Yours, if only you dare," he grinned, and uncoiled lazily. He held the shiny apple before me, glistening with the juices of fame, and I hungered to taste.

I said:

> The first snake.
> With scales of gold.

His loins bound to the earth.

His life complete.

My voice seemed to deepen, to strengthen, as my self-created devil gave me the power to change Kimminov's holy Edenic ramblings into my own poetic cries against the injustices of Eden. I no longer looked down. I looked up and saw clear through the ceiling into the sky. In my poems, Adam bit willfully into the apple. He would have no more of the heavenly whisper, "Thou shalt not." "I shall," he declared, and gladly departed from paradise to till his fields and make his poems.

It was sublime. I spoke, and, lo, they listened. The fang of the viper had struck deeply. They were as attentive as during the holiest of Torah readings. They were mine.

Only two faces showed anything other than delighted respect and admiration. One was my father's. It was confused, as when there was a mistake he couldn't find in his accounts. He chewed his underlip and glanced uselessly upward as if in expectation of an answer from the celestial bookkeeper. He had seen some of my poems, but these were new, invented as I went along from the foundations of Kimminov's; still there must have been something in my expressions that sounded familiar. If a father can't recognize his son's words, who can?

Maybe a teacher. Reb Tellman also looked quizzical. The line of his dark eyebrows arched into a *V*, and a scowl passed over his face. He leaned forward in his seat, waiting to pounce, to catch the error he knew had to come.... He knew. I don't know how he knew, but he knew all right. Still, he would not dare to interrupt. He would chafe and burn, but he would wait until the reading was over to expose me. Then he could have his day; I didn't care as long as I could continue.

The knowledge that I was doomed made me reckless. With nothing to lose, I took another bite of the apple and abandoned any pretense of taking my poems from Kimminov's. I ignored the old man completely. His voice was the wind. I conjured up a vision of my tattered notebook, opened to page one, and then, as if it were the Torah, I began to read from it, and not once did I need to ask for help. My voice rang out my own poems with my own words in my own rhythms, my own vision taking the souls of the people of Proszowice for a flight out of the tiny shul into space, and then returning them safely to tremble in their pews. Kimminov continued to recite his poetry to me, as I recited mine to the world.

Then came the reception. People sipped tea and pretended they were elegant. Delicacies of every sort were offered to the honored guest, but he merely shook his head and smiled and kissed the hands of the ladies and instructed me to tell them that their cuticles were more delicious than any pastry. Once, when I started to move away, the pock-marked old hand reached out like a talon and held me close.

The Rabbi himself congratulated me on my rendering.

My father nodded seriously and looked at me as if he had not seen me in twenty years and were trying to remember my name.

One of the many who had complimented Kimminov put his ear to the great mouth, looked puzzled, and explained, "Mr. Kimminov says that the young boy did such an excellent job that he hopes he will not refuse to continue the task, although the words of such an old man are hardly worth the voice of youth."

Kimminov was grinning like an idiot.

In that moment I felt I was the possessor of a hidden power, like Rothschild. It was not the ecstasy of my reading, but a sensation of absolute calm and dominion.

Then Reb Tellman elbowed his way through the crowd. He had an evil smirk on his face, an executioner's smile showing through the black hood. He burst out, "I thought I had read all of your poems, sir. I admire them, but I was not familiar with these. Which collection are they in?"

I felt the trap give way, and I swung free.

Then there was the sudden shock of breath in my ear, a fuming and snorting like a horse, and the tickle of the coarse gray beard. "Tell him that they were new poems."

I was still translator, still in control. I could say whatever I wanted. Kimminov need never know.

I said, "They were n——," when the words stuck in my throat. Later, my father told me that I looked like a fish brought out of the water. My heart beat as fast as a bird's. My blood was as cold as a snake's. I looked at the poet.

He was smiling innocently. Just because he could not speak did not mean that he could not hear. He had heard Reb Tellman quite well. He had also listened to my entire reading of my own works in his name.

"Not in your usual style," Reb Tellman persisted.

I did not dare to look at the poet again. I was ready for any mortification.

He whispered, "No doubt you refer to my poem about the viper."

I was stunned, silent, when a gentle poke made me jump nearly out of my shoes. "Tell them."

"No doubt you refer to my poem about the viper." My voice was that of a dead man.

"Yes," Reb Tellman snorted with derision. "Among others. In fact it was from that poem on."

Everyone seemed to be looking down on me, a circle forming. They would take out rulers, every one of them, any second, and I shrank beneath the anticipated pain. Still I found the strength to repeat the new words whispered to me by my sole companion in the circle. "Yes. . . . It was a new style for me too. . . . A new direction."

They were toying with me, Reb Tellman, the Rabbi, Kimminov himself orchestrating this public humiliation. Only my father wore a sorrowful expression which said that I had gotten myself into this, and that he could not help me. I burned with shame and anger. I had not meant to insult them, but I was not sorry. It was just that on this, my first public appearance, my own work took precedence. For this presumption I would accept punishment, but not degradation. Let the guns be readied and aimed. I would refuse the blindfold, the last cigarette. I myself would give the order to fire.

Reb Tellman was insisting on more information.

Kimminov was giggling now, like a three-month-old baby. He thought this was so funny, he did; well, I would show him. I had read my words for him once; I would again. As soon let them kill me for a whale as a guppy. With new bravura I answered, "Maybe not as refined as some of his earlier work, but with undeniable spirit."

And Kimminov broke into strange, muted, hysterical laughter. He was bent double, shaking. I could have strangled him on the spot.

Then I noticed that Reb Tellman looked as furious as I felt. He thought I was still speaking for the poet. He choked back his bile, and admitted, "Yes, but when did you write them?"

Kimminov, between sobs of delight, managed to gasp to me, "Tell them."

So I did. "They were written quite recently." And forged bravely, blindly, ahead. "None of them has yet been published. . . . But I am certain you will agree that they are up to my finest work of years past."

Reb Tellman gave a last desperate pleading look at Kimminov, but the poet, with tears in his eyes, was beyond sight. Reb Tellman nodded curtly, spun on his heel, and left the room.

Someone said, "Now what was that about?"

Nobody knew the answer, and moreover, nobody cared. The reception continued.

Finally I found the vast willpower I needed to look up at Kimminov with a question in my eyes, if not my speechless mouth:

Why? Was I simply too small, too insignificant to hurt? Was it the humor he so obviously found in the situation? Why?

"One poet to another," he whispered, and left me with the single word "snake" and a merry wink. An hour later, his carriage repaired, he went on to Cracow to collect the Prix de Lettres of the Polish Academy.

virginity

t was a bitterly cold day, unseasonable for October, and the women of Proszowice formed an ungainly line outside the ritual bath. The mikvah was a small brown structure with steam escaping like smoke between its dark wood planks. The women stamped their feet, rubbed their rough hands, and pulled their woolen shawls tight around them. Some gossiped, some did not, but all kept an eye on the bath, and the minute a body exited through the solid oaken door another body rushed to enter, and the rest inched forward over the rivulets of condensed water that ran past them and then froze.

Inside the mikvah . . . who could tell? There the distaff side ruled supreme. Men and soon-to-be-men like myself were banned from this place where mysterious feminine arcana were revealed by mother to daughter beneath the fluids of matronly virtue. I could only pass innocently beside their shrinking queue—look, listen, and wonder.

When Shivka Bellet left the mikvah, her face exuding ruddy, open-pored good health, and Selma Rabinovitch slipped inside, the first place in line was taken by an obese, red-haired tomato. This was Rebecca. Nobody knew her last name; everyone said she had forfeited her right to any respectable last name. Her parents had disowned her, and certainly no man would marry her. Rebecca was our whore.

From the other end of town the Rabbi's wife arrived, carrying a fresh towel and soap with which to purify herself before the Shabbos. Despite her elevated position, she stepped to the rear of the line, but once there, she tapped the woman in front of her on the shoulder and said, "Excuse me, but the Rabbi is waiting for me. May I step ahead of you?"

"Yes. Yes. My best wishes to yourself and the Rabbi for the holiday," Mrs. Horowitz promptly answered, and then nudged her eldest, unmarried daughter, "Let the Rebbitzen through."

The Rabbi's wife nodded at the expected privilege, tapped the next woman, and made the same request. She did this, woman by woman, until only Rebecca the whore remained between her and the warmth of the interior. The enormous slut stood in a wide, masculine stance, about to hoist her heavy legs over the threshold.

"Excuse me," said the Rabbi's wife, "but may I step ahead of you? The Rabbi is waiting for me."

Rebecca turned and boldly scrutinized our local social lioness. "So what?" she answered. "The whole town is waiting for me."

It is true that ours was a very spiritual community, but nonetheless the flesh is weak, and just as there was a place for two grocers and three tailors, there was also a place for one whore. Shocking, but there she was and she made a living. She bought chickens from the butcher, pumpernickel raisin bread from the baker, exotically scented soaps and sundries from the pharmacist, and from my father's oddly stocked general store she bought herring, utensils, and fabric, yards and yards of it to swathe her tremendous frame. My mother might have refused to serve her, but a born merchant's natural frugality and, I think, a secret pity, prevailed, and she merely refused to allow my father to wait upon the floozy. Scandalous as her orders were, they were extremely profitable, for Rebecca always demanded imported sardines, pitted olives, and the finest Persian lace. Never mind that her clothes instantly turned shabby, that her fine perfumes took on the scent of the livery, that her very presence could sour cream; as long as she insisted on an immodestly tight fit that would split seams, we would sell to her. Despite her many outrages to the public sensibility, mitigated only by her willingness to pay for them in ready cash, Rebecca was also a Jew. She attended religious services, and before doing so she cleansed herself with the rest of the women (although it was commonly conceded that she had more sins to cleanse away than most.)

Rebecca slept in a room in back of Veselka's Tavern, where the Polish drovers and horsetraders drank. Rumor had it that she went with these men, but nobody was willing to believe that, even of her. Being a Jew, she could not possibly have carnal relations with a goy, but which of the stooped holy men in shul snuck behind the tavern was also unknown. Being Jews, they could not possibly have carnal relations with a harlot. Yet there she was, in the flesh, abundantly. This paradox dominated the backstairs conversations of the eighth grade as much as did the question of how Cain and Abel could have met their wives if they were the only children of Adam and Eve.

The other boys whispered, and I knew this had to do with the strange and forbidden subjects that formed the undercurrent of the normally placid sea of Proszowice life. I could sometimes feel that current tugging at me, but I was still ignorant of its more vulgar details. I had been to a few weddings, and even participated unofficially in one, but I found them uninformative spectacles, the public ceremony merely the culmination of darksome private concerns. What little I knew I learned because I had big ears. Through walls and curtains they heard about dowries before marriage and scandals after. Still the essence of these connubial horrors was unclear to me, and I simply could not understand why such matters, whatever they were, were secret if everyone except me knew about them.

I am not talking about love. That I knew. I loved my parents. In retrospect I would realize that I loved my people. There had even been a certain young lady whom I had wooed, but that was mimicry. Love is an abstract cloak of need, while the unnamed fabric in the marital garment was so real that its very mention would evoke it from the nether regions. If it had been suggested to me in connection with my one brief fling, I probably would have struck the person perverse enough to say such a thing. Then I saw Rebecca and, how shall I put it, my body responded. First-hand, I understood the magic of lust.

It began as a tickling easily becalmed by shifting in my seat or crossing my legs, but this appeasement did not suffice for long. Furtively, I let my wrist graze myself, but this only inflamed the odd sensation. The itch, all the more irritating because I could not scratch, grew in strength and pulsed to drown out the more rapid beating of my heart. It became the preoccupation of my young

life. In school, at home, and—God, blessed be He, forgive me—
at worship, I prayed for more than I had any right to.

The worst bedevilments came at night. Alone in my bed, I
could not find the distractions of the day. I tossed and turned, and
in my fevered dreams the feathers I slept on became a voluptuous
fleshy beast crowned by my headboard of red hair. The blazing
tendrils tied me fast, while the great, doughy woman seemed to
absorb me. Still, at the crucial moment my imagination failed me.
I knew the location of the difficulty and gathered that it was
similarly positioned in the feminine gender but was differently
constructed, complementary—but how? In the morning I padded,
exhausted, out to the kitchen, to find my mother and father. He
sipped coffee, she tea, before setting off to pray and to work. They
asked me if I wasn't feeling well.

I might have thought so myself. I was still not certain what
cure I needed, but intuitively I knew that Rebecca was the only
doctor for me. If it was bones that were broken, she could mend
them, and if my mind was ravaged by its own phantoms, she could
dispel them, and was even better suited to resolve my pubescent
dilemma. She was a pagan goddess with exaggerated bust and
buttocks, a walking, breathing fertility symbol. From the second
I chanced to overhear her comeback to the forces of responsible
abstinence outside the mikvah I craved her with all my adolescent
zeal. I could suddenly read the progress of many of the previous
year's heretofore inexplicable feelings to this last, I thought, climactic
chapter in my development into a man.

After school I found every imaginable excuse to pass by Veselka's
Tavern, hoping for a glimpse of Rebecca through the frosted windows. More often than not she was in her back room, the mere
thought of which nearly made me faint. On legs brittle as dead
birches, I staggered off to try other possible disreputable stamping
grounds. Alas, like the tavern, all of them—the stables, the mill,
and the hotel—were also beyond the proper boundaries that cir-
cumscribed the life of a tiny Jewish boy. I had to rely on the
vagaries of randomly crossed paths. I saw her on the streets, and

I saw her bulky shadow behind the translucent *mechitza* that separated the sexes in our shul. The pale, insubstantial curtain seemed to extend beyond the aisle into the world, where it became an unbridgeable chasm. I wracked my brain for a way to approach her, but to no avail. All of my tactics and strategies were foredoomed, except on Friday afternoon. Then, wrapped in a towel the size of a flag, her heavy, fleshy calves beneath, her gladiatorial shoulders above, she stood with the other women in front of the mikvah.

"Hussy!" they scoffed, and I envied them their closeness to the object of their unjust disdain.

I pitied Rebecca, but I need not have. "Don't get noble with me," she retorted. "You all sell yourselves. In fact, I'm the only one free not to. I'm the only one beholden to me."

In the background, I was delirious. My interpretation of "free not to" read "free to," with anyone—i.e., me. I might have run to her ample arms right there had it not been for the presence of the other women of Proszowice. Everyone from Leah Horowitz to the Rabbi's wife was there. My own mother stood there in a similar towel, and the very thought of *her* calves drove me tearfully from the scene.

Rebecca wasn't in synagogue the next day, and I didn't see her until almost a week later. It was perhaps four o'clock, already dusk at that time of year. I had come home from school the long way, via an empty Veselka's, and I was looking after our store for my father, who was studying. I was sitting on top of the ladder near the canned goods, where I kept a volume of Byron translated into Yiddish, when the door creaked wide. There was something about the decisive solidity of the approaching steps that caught my attention. As I hastened down the ladder, my left foot hooked into a rung, I tripped, and fell at her mud-flecked red shoes, surprisingly petite for the weight they supported. "At your service," I said with all the suavity I could muster from the floor.

"I want my shoes shined, I'll go to the bootblack," she snapped. "Get me a bolt of chenille, the pink, seven yards. Deliver it to the seamstress." She threw a gold piece toward the counter and was gone before it landed.

I had seldom viewed the precious metal before. I remembered the sound of Isaac the Millionaire's good-luck ruble as glorious but tinny in comparison to the rich, earthy tone of Rebecca's as it spun, wobbled, and fell as flat as a drunkard on its face. Her money was smudged, with a rim of tar surrounding the king's profile, whereas Isaac kept his as clean as his spectacles. His was a charm, but this was coin of the realm. It stared at me like a golden eye imbedded on the wooden countertop, mesmerizing. I knew what I should do. I should call my mother, tell her of this great purchase, and give her the coin to hide as she saw fit. I opened my mouth, but no words came out. The coin had stolen my voice and was dictating my actions. I reached out for the poisoned lure.

A minute later my mother came in. "Did I hear someone?"

"No," I said. "I mean just me. I tripped over the ladder."

"Did you hurt yourself? That ladder's dangerous."

More than the ladder was dangerous. I felt myself back on it, balancing precariously, with the heady, overripe smell of Rebecca wafting through my mind. Part of me wanted to shout "Stop!" before it was too late to admit that she had come in and bought the fabric; but then it was too late, and I could no longer recant. By then the gold coin in my pocket was as much a part of me as my memory. I felt it bulge so that anyone, everyone, could see it, my own personal mark of Cain. Was I my father's store's keeper? I carefully taped off seven yards of the nubby bolt of chenille, added seven inches for good measure, and carried it to the seamstress, my fingers kneading a small sweat stain in the corner.

Luckily the seamstress didn't notice. She complained instead about the sittings to come. "Seven yards! She doesn't want a dress. She wants a tent."

That night I dreamed of the Palestinian desert.

I knew that the gold piece was the equivalent of Rebecca's soul, not to mention her favors, so I kept it with me at all times. It was an icicle in my pocket, freezing and burning in biting concert, but I would not remove it. I was afraid that someone might find it and guess the secret already written on my face (I did not think that anyone would miss the fabric that had lain dust-gathering above the buttons for years). But, more importantly, it was a palpable token of the lady's affection. I might have been a medieval knight, wearing her favor tied to my lance, were it not for the vow of secrecy I had sworn in order to protect her honor. With no justification whatsoever, I knew it was still there, resplendent under the dingy lace.

Moshele Rosen disagreed with me.

"She what?" I said.

Moshele repeated himself.

"That's not true."

Moshele could not understand my objection. I might as well have disputed the nature of birds, claiming, "They do not fly." He ignored me.

I punched him in the stomach. If I had thought, I would have anticipated an awkward, bearish tussle, but Moshele merely clutched himself and bent double, looking up at me with pain and surprise.

I was called before Reb Tellman.

"He used a bad word," I explained.

"Certainly he shouldn't have, but neither have you been anointed the Lord's own avenging angel." His tiny eyes glittered, and I wondered if he was one of the men who had contributed to the gold piece in my pocket. I wondered if he would have agreed with Moshele if he had known whom the bad word referred to. Who, I wanted to know, anointed all Proszowice the Lord's avengers?

Reb Tellman's stiff meterstick came crashing down on my bare knuckles. There was a thin pink outline of a hand on the blonde wood table, but I hardly noticed. I was so in thrall to the notion of Rebecca that the afflictions of the world became as small in my eyes as she was large. Everything about her, from her charming, Chinese princess feet to the fire of red hair she tossed as she walked, further bewitched me. Every word from the Torah reading on "the fleshpots of Sodom," every insinuating teenage leer, every lover's glance, every innocuous everything, had but one frame of reference for me. All, seen through my Rebecca's bright green eyes, had to do with the one magnificent new quality in my universe: sex.

Unfortunately my access to the object of my prematurely prurient vision was severely limited. Her dress was out of my grubby little hands and she had ordered enough canned specialties to last for months, so there was virtually no chance of another visitation to our store. Neither, I gathered, was she doing business with the other merchants, nor much with Veselka. She seemed to have retreated in moody solitude to her single back room. Oh, how I wished to comfort her—almost as much as I longed for her to comfort me. I tried to find more appropriate inamoratas, but the breastless girls of my age satisfied neither my imagination nor my incarnation. No, only my newly withdrawn scarlet woman would serve. I choked at the thought of her pursuing her chosen profession, but I swallowed my discontent because that was the only way to unlock the door to the house of her ill repute. After all, I had the key in my pocket.

It was the first day of Hanukkah. Contrary to our usual Jewish tendency to be mournful, this is a party of a holiday, a holiday for happiness's sake. The prayers are minimal, the festivities extravagant. There are holiday foods and holiday songs. Off in the corner, we children spun our dreidels, competing for chocolates and our Hanukkah booty. Perhaps it was the zloties I was winning and losing that put me in mind of the true fortune I had pressing reassuringly on my thigh. Perhaps it was the family gathering that put me in mind of my personal lack. Perhaps it was the shape of the squatly spinning top that put me in mind of Rebecca. I rose unsteadily to my feet and announced that I was going for a walk.

"But it's so cold out," my mother said.

I put on my winter coat, my scarf, and my fur-lined, red-checked cap. Bundled up like a sack of laundry, I did a penguin step into the night. I knew every house, every brick, every brightly lit window with the first day of Hanukkah's candle burning inside its wooden frame. These were my neighbors, my friends, my people; but there was something about the circumstances of my nocturnal stroll that made them strange. Heading toward the other part of town, past the blacksmith's forge, the dairy barn, the cheder, I felt as if I was leaving forever. The gold coin weighed me down as much as a suitcase. The wind began to whip the ends of my scarf. My feet landed uncomfortably in the ruts they had worn over the years in the roadway. Its direction seemed subtly altered.

I passed the women's mikvah and the men's, and then I realized where I was going. I knew that the purity restored by the ritual bath would never be mine. Instead of its cleansing waters, it was the muck of sin I was immersing myself in. Up to and beyond the neck, I was drowning in sin, and still I pursued it. I could not resist. On this joyous night that should have been an affirmation of traditional values, I would plunge into the abyss. The Hanukkah candles would signal the beginning of a downward path to shame and depravity. Several months from now I would become a Bar Mitzvah under false pretenses; I would enter my majority with my glorious birthright bankrupt, sold for a more transitory, more reprehensible gratification than Esau's bowl of pottage.

I would change my name for my family's sake; I would spare them that last indignity, as Rebecca had hers years before. There were people in Proszowice who remembered Rebecca growing up, a shy girl, they said, growing and growing, the cruel butt of her classmates' jokes, and continuing to grow, and finding her vengeance in her own self-destruction. Would I be her male counterpart, her pimp? I could see myself in a gruesome syphilitic wallow, but if this was what all my religious and literary longings had brought me to, so be it. I took the pen with the bloody ink and signed away my soul in return for the one single pleasure that was more necessary to me than all of God's future.

The lights from Veselka's Tavern cast a red glow outside. I worried briefly that somebody might see me, but then I realized that no respectable person would come within a mile of such a place on such a night. I was beyond the pale. I inhaled the earthy smell of horses and smoke and heavy Polish food cooked in lard. I put my mittened hand to my forehead in salute and peered through the window. Rebecca was sitting on a bar stool, her legs spread apart and hooked onto the lower rungs like stirrups. She was wearing the pink chenille gown for me. The gown was not cinched anywhere; it flowed over and disguised the enormity of her figure. I was enchanted.

Also in the bar were Veselka, a few customers, and Magda, Rebecca's friend and coworker. Magda was a nasty, skinny girl who stole from our store and spat at my father and called him "Jew." As I opened the door she instantly turned on me.

"What do you want, Samson?" I think this was a reference to the sidelocks that poked out from beneath my cap.

"Leave him be," Rebecca said. "It must be about something I ordered. If anything's wrong just put it on my account."

My hand clutched the gold piece like a stone. My fingernails curled and bit into my palm. I thrust the clenched fist forward and, unable to speak, nonverbal idiot, opened it. The coin seemed to suck all of the lights in the room to its shining surface.

"What do you . . . ah haaa!" Rebecca understood.

Veselka eyed me with drunken malevolence while Magda turned away to sip a distasteful-looking amber liquid.

"I should," Rebecca said, musing aloud. "I really should. Both for the money, worth how much? say, seven yards of chenille, and to put them in their place. Laugh at me, will they, treat me like dirt, then their holy children come begging. I should take it," she repeated. And then she looked at me, really looked at me for the first time. "Aw, get out of here. I'm old enough to be your . . ."

she reached out and shut her hand around my hand around the coin and squeezed so that my bones seemed to crack. "Scram!"

I spent most of the night in the lurid glare of the tavern lights. I stood in the cold watching Rebecca perched like a boulder on the flimsy bar stool. She bantered with the customers and accepted a drink from one who limped across the floor to make his offer. They exchanged words, his lips twitching suggestively, her head thrown back, then bent forward in sly explanation. In order to hear her I forewent the pleasure of watching her and pressed my tender left ear to the frosty windowpane.

The world spun like a dreidel. I thought it was my home, or even the synagogue I was listening in on. Just like my father or the Rabbi, Rebecca the whore was actually recounting the legend of Hanukkah for the nonbelievers. She was the only Jew they would tolerate in their bar, precisely because she had brought her religion as low as they were, yet she persisted in her recitation. She told them of the Maccabees' fight for independence, of their conquest of Jerusalem, and of their last drop of oil, and how it burned for eight days.

Veselka scoffed. "Fairy tales. Fit for the long hairs."

"Eh, you think you can make your candle last eight days? Eight minutes is more like it," she laughed with a harsh bray.

Because I did not understand the joke, I was not bent double along with the rest of her audience when Rebecca's face underwent its first change. She stopped in mid-laugh, her lips curling back from her teeth in an animal grimace my stomach felt through the wall. Her face went through a dozen quick contortions in half as many seconds and then, abruptly, calmed. She went on laughing, but with an uncharacteristic restraint, and then she excused herself, and I left.

Trudging gloomily back through the snow and slush, past the houses with the first forlorn Hanukkah candle in each window, I thought of writing Rebecca one of the letters I had become famous for. That would show her how adult I was, I thought, knowing all along that it would never happen because, whatever her many wonderful qualities, my dear Rebecca was simply not a reader. I yearned to ride a horse, or shoe one, or do something, anything to impress her and penetrate the barrier that stood between us.

Over the days of the holiday, as the number of candles in every Jewish window increased, I watched my sweet Sheba's pain grow accordingly. A twinge starting at the base of her spine would arch upward and emerge from the broken mirror of her face. This occurred more and more often; still, none of her companions seemed to notice, or maybe they just didn't care. There she was, a beautiful, billowing canvas of a woman waiting to give a home to a lucky man like myself, and all they wanted was shelter for the night, the louts!

My three-hundred-pound angel was not at all well. I wondered if I should take it upon myself to call the doctor, but I remembered my last ill-advised overture and decided that I should continue to admire her from afar. Every torture that wracked her darling wanton's countenance I felt as she did, but I dared not intrude. I thought that perhaps her trouble was, as mine for her, for me, then I realized that somewhere in my sympathy I had lost my agony. I cared more for her than for myself.

Then she disappeared.

It was the last day of Hanukkah. Rebecca's convulsions were so regular you could tell time by them, and I was nearly frantic with worry. She was not in Veselka's or any of her other usual haunts; she was simply gone—where, I hadn't a clue. All I knew was her absence, which was a vacuum devouring everything but my fear.

After a dinner that I could scarcely force down, I snuck out of our house, in search. A light rain had fallen and frozen into a shiny crust. Now empty of moisture, the air was so clear it practically crackled. The eight sacred glittering candles in each window in which I sought my Rebecca seemed physical entities delineated from the palpable dark through which I moved like a ghost. If not for the anxiety that drove me relentlessly on, huffing and puffing the only clouds in the sky, it would have been a spectacular evening. It was getting late, but I could not go home. My parents would worry, but if I returned to soothe them they would not let me out again, and I had to find her. I was on a quest.

I peeked into the room in the back of the tavern. It was small and housed a narrow, roughly used bed with a tangle of silk sheets strewn across it. There was a single dresser with an oval mirror in front of which was drawn up an army of cans, bottles, tubes, and crystals containing who knew what exotic feminine lotions. Through the glazed window the room exuded an air of sultry decadence both enticing and repulsive.

I had looked everywhere, and was at my wit's end when I finally summoned up the courage to return to Veselka's. I hesitated on the doorstep before the noose of a New Year's wreath before I recalled the tantalizing image that had drawn me there, sucked in a lungful of cold air, and pushed open the portals of hell.

"Shut the door before we all freeze!" A wave of hostility engulfed me.

I stammered, "Where's Rebecca?"

Magda spun around from the bar. "And won't I do?" she smirked. In a saucy holiday mood, she pulled down the corner of her dress and offered me her thin breast. It was so much less substantial than the bounty I would have imagined to lie beneath Rebecca's chenille, had I had the nerve to imagine. It was a scrawny, ugly thing, but I could not stop staring at its one brown spot, like the Cyclops's eye.

"Where's Rebecca?" I repeated to the nipple, my voice strained as a piano wire.

Beasts of prey, my distress made them meaner. "So only the big Mama will do," Magda laughed.

"Where is she?" I was nearly crying.

"Try your precious Rabbi's house. I think she needs advice." And she and everyone else laughed at me, and worse, at my Rabbi, and worst of all, at Rebecca.

Veselka pawed at the still dangling breast.

Suddenly afraid of being caught and overcome by the alcohol fumes, I ran to the door. Once outside, however, I took Magda's sarcastic counsel and set off for Alter Street, where the Rabbi and Rebbitzen were fast asleep. As they had been the first to light this final holiday night's candles precisely at sundown, their eight commemorative flames were down to the stumps.

I had the queer presence of mind to notice that, given the rate at which different candles burned and given the time at which they were lit, some had gone out while others continued to wax proudly. Some menorahs had only seven candles burning, and some had six. Every minute another blinked out at the edge of my vision. The sky seemed to be pressing downward, and the stars to be vanishing along with the flickering Jewish fires. Some menorahs had only five candles burning, and some had four. Ominous shadows extended into the public square like pools of quicksand. The bricks and wood seemed to breathe, and I thought I heard the clanking of chains not far away. Some menorahs had only three candles burning and some had two. I felt so small, so isolated, so helpless.

As the last candles in the menorahs were guttering out and I was about to surrender to the cruel decree of misfortune, a cry split the midnight.

The clarion burst faded as abruptly as it came, leaving only the nervous tingling in my spine to give it credence. Then a soft moaning floated through the streets, and I followed it like the aroma of fresh-baking bread. Concentrating entirely on the sound, which wavered above and below the point of audibility, I crossed the threatening square and passed by the eerily creaking eaves of the shul. I barely noticed where I was going, wherever the keening whisper led me. It was so faint that I had to still my own heartbeat to grasp each frail note on the wing. Winding a tortuous path through the village sidestreets on my panther's feet, I followed until the threnody finally came to a stop. I was alone at the mouth of a dark alley, toward which an electric impulse suddenly pulled me. I ran, stumbled, and plowed clumsily through to the end. There was the women's mikvah, still radiating warmth from the day.

I heard nothing, I saw nothing, but I walked straight ahead and entered. If my father or Reb Tellman or the Rabbi had seen me dare to go so far as to touch this building dedicated to the women of Proszowice I would have incurred, and well deserved, the beating of my life—though my motives were as pure as the women who bathed there. The moment I opened the door, I heard a harsh intake of breath. An awful span later, the breath was exhaled.

"Rebecca?"

She laughed, a terrible cackle. "My prince," and her laughter turned involuntarily to sobs. "Get out," she hissed. "Leave me alone."

"No," I said, amazed at my audacity. "You need me." I stepped forward and fell over a bench. I was where no man had ever been. The floor was damp. I crawled.

I touched something soft and let my fingers wander until they recoiled, as if of their own volition; it was skin. It was warm and elastic and, well, you certainly know, but I don't think I had ever touched a girl before, and doubtless not with intimacy. I sat as still as a rock while the person I touched went through a spasm that shook the wooden floor in the dark. I took off my scarf and wiped her forehead, which was drenched with perspiration.

A moonbeam came through a chink in the roof's shingles and lit on Rebecca's tearful face. Her mouth drooped, her eyes rolled up nearly under her brow. Before a cloud passed over my heavenly lamp, I caught a glimpse of the rest of her body, for she had shed her clothes like an animal. Her massive breasts swayed back and forth with her contortions. One leg was bent, the other splayed outward, and I saw a rag of pink chenille beneath her. Most shocking, her stomach protruded in a perfect dome, like the mosque I had seen in the sepia-tinted lithograph of Jerusalem that hung over my family's hearth.

Then the contractions began again, and after that I didn't have time to think or light to observe. I simply acted. I followed Rebecca's lead. When she wanted to bend forward I helped her bend; when her body grew slack I eased her down. I mopped her when I could and held her when I had to. Her bulk heaved and strained in my slight hands, and our sweat intermingled as the work grew more and more strenuous. Her muffled shrieks and my panting accompaniment composed a symphony of breath that peaked and subsided, peaked and subsided, in deliriously rapid succession. Finally, the quakes were one minute apart, each following on the barely dissipated wake of the one before, when the blood began to flow, and I put a piece of the chenille robe's empty sleeve into Rebecca's mouth so that she would not bite through her tongue.

We were in the center of a basin, surrounded by rows of benches above which were hooks for the women's towels. A tiny piece of soap that someone had forgotten shone like a little moon in the corner of the basin beside an inch of still water.

The head came out first and a peculiar thrill ran through me. I took hold of the body, slick with a membrane like the white of an uncooked egg, and I pulled. Simultaneously, the baby popped free and a strange, ecstatic discharge burst from my loins. I hadn't known that this was what I had been waiting for all those difficult weeks and years, but the second it occurred I knew: this was sex.

Thus with the consummation of my earthly passion I was initiated into the mysteries of life, and the child I would always think of as my own came into the world. I had heard rumors to the effect that sex creates babies, but I had been under the impression that it wouldn't be so immediate a consequence of Rebecca's and my divine union. It was spectacular all right, but it was also grueling, and I understood why there weren't more babies around. I didn't think I would want to do this again for a long time.

Pale, haggard Rebecca reached out for our child. I do not know whether her behavior was instructed or instinctive, but she severed the cord that still connected her and the baby. She wiped its face with the loose fleshy part of her elephantine underarm, and with the power of that arm she gave it a solid thwack. Its mouth blew open. I could hear the dramatic intake of breath, like wind rushing through a crack in a wall. It was a boy. He cried and she fell back. I took the youngster in my arms and rocked him until he slept.

NURSERIES

*R*hymes, riddles—children like these. They offer a special, penetrating view of the adult world, like a peek at the body beneath the clothes or the skeleton through the skin. They offer mystery and revelation, and secret, suggestive levels of thought. But like that other treasury of double meaning, the Caballa, a joke's hidden truth may be perceived only by an initiate. For example, "What grows smaller as it grows older?"

My little sister stood unsteadily, her fingers wrapped around the bars of her cage like plump sausages. She drooled enthusiastically.

"A candle," I answered.

She stretched out a miniature hand to spread across my face.

"A candle," I repeated, as her fingers explored my teeth and gums the way a blind man reads a statue. "You know, when it's lit, it melts."

She fell backward, her feet bicycling the air with glee.

It wasn't that funny, but I was glad to be appreciated. I did not mention that a candle may also be snuffed out by the breath of God.

"Here's another. What grows larger when you take the head away from it? You don't know? You can't guess? A pillow. That's because it puffs up. Hey, I've got a million of them."

It was the season for children. Other times had seen foreigners, rabbis, beggars, newlyweds, but this year's autumn was teeming with young. There was a new Kleiner and a typically ruddy, moon-faced Bobover; and, of course, there was the son of Rebecca, held proudly through a chorus of shame. We were as fruitful as the tropics; to find an exact number, multiply. Compared to the late-comers, my baby sister was a grandam.

She had appeared at the start of the previous spring, like the first crocus. It was a trick of enormous magnitude, and I had reason to believe that my mother was the magician. Locked in a room with only Helga the midwife to assist her, she brought forth. Unfortunately, the peanut under the unsuspected shell is wonderful not because it is a peanut, so my sister rapidly lost her novel charm. For six months, she was more like a loaf of unbaked bread than a member of the family. Lying in the corner of the kitchen with her doughy, unformed features, it was a miracle that somebody didn't put her in the oven.

Gradually, her cheekbones rose and her cheeks sunk. A gray thatch covered most of her scalp. I supposed she was just a late bloomer. Now she was giggling, crawling, taking her first steps, and shaping her first words. "Mmmm . . . aaaa." It sounded like a cross between a cow and a sheep, "Mooo . . . Baaa," although barn-yard babies were far more clever.

My parents were blind to the bad qualities of their offspring. Take my brother. No matter his clumsiness or stupidity, just let the intellectual athlete recite the ten commandments while hanging upside down from a branch and the folks would fairly swoon. They even found satisfaction in my adventures; but they went too far when they transformed the most odious products of my sister's laxity into golden nuggets. To look at my mother changing her diaper you might have thought the task an honor.

"How can you smile when you're doing something so disgusting?"

"You don't think this is poetic?" She raised my sister's legs like a chicken's for the dressing.

"Not extremely."

"Well," she said, "I did the same for you, and now look at the fine young gentleman I have," and she deftly swabbed the pink bottom.

"You're kidding!"

She lowered the squirming carcass. "Ask your father."

"Daddy?" I could not recall a time when I had not existed, so I must have been eternal, and since I could not exist without awareness, I must have been omniscient. (There was a fallacy in this theory, but don't ask me where.) I pled for confirmation of my self as I knew me. "Daddy?"

He answered, "What walks on four legs in the morning, two in the afternoon, and three at night?"

Remember, you are listening to a person who has aspired to the estate of wings and wheels. If two legs were a hindrance to my dreams, imagine the burden of a third and, retrospectively, a fourth. Yes, a short month before I had been prone to actions that I now recollected with a blush, but still! Mine was the soul to inherit the hallowed realms of poesy, not gibberish.

My father saw my crestfallen expression. "It's not so bad," he tried to soothe me. "Everything ages. Goats. Trees. Stones. It's a natural phenomenon, the same with nations as well as people. The Greeks, for example, were in their prime when they made up that riddle."

I thought of the spare, noble lines of a Greek temple and the marble goddess within. Then I thought of the Proszowice shul, like an outhouse, and the old men who practically lived there, and my sister's first public appearance; it had been early the summer before. Everyone was shiny with sweat. She was uncomfortable, but as long as she remained in the women's section her stuttering infant sounds mixed well with the matronly cooing around her, the gossip, and a little prayer. The serious old men were like crows pecking at their books. After worship, though, they lifted their heads and came over to peer at the unwrinkled one. Their hovering shadows must have disturbed her, because she began to wake up. Her leg flipped out of my mother's grasp into my eye. It stung *me,* yet *she* bawled.

"What lungs!" someone joked. "Yes, she'll make a fine wife," another replied; and they pressed closer to rub her chin with veiny forefingers. The mass of elders, angling and jostling for a view, plowed into my poor mother.

"Don't drop her, now," the Rabbi said.

My mother turned a withering glare at this giver of well-intentioned advice. She would sooner put her hand in a guillotine than drop the fleshy burden. I pushed the foot out of my face.

Everything ages, I thought. So not only was I personally vulnerable; my whole race was a doddering wreck. It was awful to contemplate, but nonetheless I had to know. "And we, the Jews?"

Here's where my father surprised me. "We're always babies," he said. "That's why we survive."

This opened up an entirely new perspective. If all Jews were babies, then Proszowice was the nursery in which we matured.

The infant self must have been a perfect outline progressively defaced by the human character. Smooth out the creases of desperation, however, remove the warts of melancholy and the discoloration of sin, and you could work the same alchemy as my parents did upon my little sister's waste. By peering backward through the telescope of time, you could make the lame walk, the atrocious gorgeous, the depraved innocent. I gave Zalman the Digger his misplaced vigor and Isaac the Millionaire his original honesty. As modeled on the image of my little sister, I surrounded myself with a community restored to the blessed state of their vestigial fourth limbs.

"What is a chicken without any bones?" I asked.

My little sister stared.

"An egg."

"Mmmm. . . ."

Her life was an endless, harmonic round of eating and sleeping, with an occasional bath to break the routine. She was played with and prayed for as if the Jewish people existed solely for her sake. In the nursery, the nurseling was all.

Greedily suckling, she knew nothing from the woe of our fathers. Then it pierced our shelter and descended. Her breath came uneasily and she woke with a fever that wet rags could not cool. She thrashed and perspired so that her few hairs stuck to her forehead in long, single strands. You could see from her wide, stricken eyes that she saw demons crouched at the foot of her crib. Taunting her, hooting and prodding, they taught the lesson of Genesis. Every bite from the tree of knowledge was a step away from the Garden.

She had the intelligence of a clam, but the nasty intuition came upon her. She was initiated into the mysteries of mortality, and suffered without rhyme or reason.

My father pounded nuts, fruits, and spices into a healing gruel, which he spoonfed the mournful child. My brother did acrobatics, and I told jokes; but she was inconsolable. She wailed with an angel's unearthly sorrow. My mother rocked the cradle and sang:

In the sky little stars burn, in the river wavelets turn.
In the window the Moon peeks, and to tads and tots it
    speaks:
"Sleep, sleep till the break of day, when the Sun comes out
    to play.
When it goes off toward night, I, in moonlight soft, recite
A sleepy fairy tale or two, as I keep watch over you . . .
Sweet slumber I bring. A hushed song I sing . . .
Sleep, sleep, sleep. Children, chipmunks, chicks, and
    sheep."

With the lullaby behind it like a breath of wind behind a ship, the household ark sailed on. My brother studied the Talmud, followed by calisthenics in the yard. My father and I tended the store, but he was preoccupied with concocting another vile remedy for his only daughter. I dreamed idly of the outside world while stacking wheels of cheese. On my mother's birthday, I bought her a bouquet.

My gift consisted of three wildflowers and one rose purchased at Medisky's greenhouse. They were bound together with a piece of red yarn from which dangled a homemade card with a poem too personal to repeat.

My mother had been awake for nearly twenty-four hours. There were calluses on her fingertips from pushing the cradle to the pulsing whimpers of her charge. She looked up past the flowers with heavy-lidded curiosity. She had forgotten her birthday. Pleased by my regard, she smiled wearily and put her cheek to mine. That touch was all I asked.

My sister's eyes lit up and her fingers uncurled. It was the first voluntary motion she had made since the fever struck. She stirred with the scent and grabbed the flowers from my mother. Her fingers played up the stem like a flute. The whimpering ceased. She stroked the petals and pressed them into her face and began to chuckle. I didn't say a word.

I sat on the fourth step of the ladder in my father's store. I think I was attempting to compose a poem on age, something to do with an hourglass and a scythe. My shoes were untied, my shirt untucked. There was the usual racket of children and customers, but I didn't care a fig. I was in the throes of artistic inspiration, and nearly jumped when hailed.

"Why there you are!" My father was by the fish counter, his white smock stained with the pink and gray pigments of his trade. He looked like a French painter. He was grinning. "You devil, you!"

"Me?"

"No," he said, "this beauty." And he bent under the ladder. For a second I thought he was lifting my shadow off the floor. I felt a rush of alarm, and then dismay. I saw the flowers the shadow was holding. Her gloom gone, my little sister had followed me out of the kitchen into the store, where she plopped herself down, legs crossed like a jade Buddha, the nosegay in her lap a pilgrim's offering.

"Hello, cockroach." My father hoisted the insect up with ease. Happy now, she gurgled like water in a barrel. She reached out to squeeze his nose with her left hand while her right crushed the rose.

Why, I wondered, was this love of children so tremendous? It was a consequence of neither pragmatics nor aesthetics, as she served no purpose and was unpleasant to think of. It was a gut feeling, pure as the gourmet's examination of a fish before dinner. It was the contemplation of experience rather than experience itself.

They began giggling together with an intimacy, or immodesty, that embarrassed me. I climbed the stepladder up to the rafters, from which strings of dried mushrooms and garlic cloves hung beside my ears. I turned my attention to the dusty swatches of fabric rolled up and tucked away by my great-grandfather before my time. They looked like the rare skins of fabulous, polka-dotted beasts.

Beyond the scrolls of material was a dark attic giving onto the beams and roof. Smoke risen through the ceiling to the enclosed vault gave it the acrid scent of an altar. Grit lay as thick as a piece of paper. There were shadowy corners that had not seen light in a hundred years. I felt like Jonah in the whale, exploring this weird, ribbed sanctuary. "You know, there's a really huge nest here," I stated.

Below me I heard goo-goos, ga-gas, and special dill pickle tickles.

"Yes, the nest of some sort of enormous insect. They seem to be burrowing into the wood." I peered intently elsewhere, but I saw through the planks my father with one leg raised, my sister bouncing on it like a marionette.

"Yes, they're etching patterns. Like letters, yes, exactly like Hebrew letters, although I can't make sense of the words."

"Really?"

"I think I've heard of these creatures. They're named alphabet bugs, not that they can actually write. It's that the original inventors of language imitated the shapes they saw in nature. Stars or waves were too complex to transcribe, but the carvings of insects represented order and definition." Now there was an elegant scientific explanation.

"Hmm."

"What does that mean?"

"Well...."

"Well what? Don't you believe me?" I could feel the hackles rising along my neck. "Do you need witnesses? Evidence?"

"To tell the truth...." He was grinning.

"If you don't believe it, you can climb up here and see for yourself." I stood and the ladder swayed, but I didn't care. I felt like the Rabbi raining damnation down onto the congregation for its lack of faith. I thought of the headfirst dive I might take and wondered whether my father would drop her to save me. "If you don't believe me, just put her down and come up here."

"No, that's not necessary." He tried to placate me.

But I had worked myself into a self-righteous fit. I would have as little of his soothing as my little sister had had before my bouquet. "No, it *is* necessary. If you don't believe me, climb. Climb!"

"All right, all right already . . . I believe you."

The storm clouds passed from my personal sky. The mist cleared. The sun shone. Of course he didn't believe me. I didn't believe that he believed me. Why should he? Enormous beetles spelling out magic formulas in the attic?

I had lied. An accessory after the fiction, my father had also lied in order to satisfy me. He lied when he said he believed me, and I completed the circle by lying when I pretended to believe that he believed me. "Deceit" was the name of this game, yet I felt as joyous as my sister when she emerged from the depths with a bunch of wildflowers and a rose.

"Riddle the riddler, fiddle-dee-dee." I was ecstatic. "I have seen a man walking, on two legs mind you, a lifeless man who never existed. How is this possible?"

A thoughtful look crossed my father's face. My sister tried to scratch her left ear with her right hand, around the back of her head.

"It was a reflection on water," I said. "Now, who is and is not, has a name, and answers a voice? You don't know? You can't guess? An echo, believe me, an echo."

Everyone here lied: for ease, for entertainment, for the sheer holy hell of it. The truth is we engaged our illusions at the expense of truth. The truth is there's no truth other than the one we create.

America, there's an image for you! Bands playing, flags waving, sparks from the forge of liberty. In America the Jews were rich. They drank tea with Rockefeller and didn't worry from Poles cudgeling them. In America the Jews dressed like Polish barons. In America a Jew could become a poet.

The synagogues in America were so tall there were sofas along the stairs for the women to rest on. There was a magnificent boulevard called Second Avenue, in the restaurants of which the Jews ate food like the tsars, except kosher, in the theaters of which they played the works of Shakespeare and Sholom Aleichem, but not on Shabbos.

Jacob Lester whispered the word as if it were sacred, "America."

Jergenchic, the barber, whipped up a lather from a soapy glass. "What about it?"

"I'm going."

"What!"

"Yes."

"When?"

"Now."

"But why?"

"Because!"

I could picture Lester on the cracked red leather chair, his black beard turned white with foam. Idly boasting, he was led by his own fancy into a resolve he could not repudiate.

The news spread like the flash of Jergenchic's scissors. With each wet curl that dropped to the floor another household was informed. Horowitz, the landlord, thrust his poxy face into my father's store and shouted, "Lester's emigrating!" My father immediately balled up his apron and called to my mother, "Lester's emigrating!"

She was more sanguine. "Again?"

"Hurry."

"All right, all right already." She was folding a towel. She turned to me. "Will you watch the baby?"

"We're all babies," I muttered. "Except Lester." I felt awe and envy and resentment at the loss this would mean to me. The one ray of enlightenment that had penetrated the Polish murk was to be extinguished.

"So, fine, so one baby to another, will you watch her?"

"Yes, yes."

"Now you know where her oatmeal is? And you know how to heat the milk? Not too hot. And the extra quilt is in the hall closet. And in case. . . ."

I thought of Lester, stupified by his rash declaration, no doubt, but thrilled with the attention it was bringing him. The more folks who came to shake the hand of the man who would shake the hand of Rockefeller, the more bound he was to his folly. He stroked his clean-shaven chin as if he had just made a decision to grow a moustache. He would book voyage within weeks. He would write letters.

"I know. I know. I know." I groaned. My sister was about as difficult to take care of as a gardenia.

Still instructing, "and a new bib is in the bottom drawer . . . ," my parents left to join the gathering crowd at the barber's.

Stuck in the nursery, I paced and chafed with jealousy. I was tired of infancy. I wanted to grow up.

My sister, meanwhile, beamed at me with a big, stupid smile. Her tongue lolled out of the corner of her mouth. She grabbed and spilled a sack of kasha. Then she spat and tried to eat a chair, but there were no major problems until she began to smear the stairs with mustard; at least I hoped it was mustard. Attending this perpetual-motion machine may not have been strenuous, but it was an ordeal. I could not imagine my mother on guard against every imminent disaster every night and every day, and she claimed to have done the same for my brother and myself.

The kid stood up with a wobble, lost her balance, and fell. Still she labored to her feet again, as though she knew that this was a trick worth mastering. She persevered like a caterpillar flicked off a porch recommencing the arduous climb, like my mother starting another child.

"Dance?" I asked. This was a favorite activity I had seen her and my father perform. I held her hands, squirming little animals, in mine and maneuvered her body across the floor.

Maybe it was dancing with an unfamiliar partner, or maybe it was my lingering resentment that changed her mood. Maybe it was clouds scudding across her private sun, but I could see her eyes darkening and feel her steps lose their bounce. She peered anxiously about, maybe for parents, maybe at demons.

"C'mon, the orchestra's just warming up."

She had no inkling of the worlds of thought and speech beyond her barnyard vocabulary. Her mouth dropped open and a long, hollow moan seeped out. It sounded like her very soul was escaping.

"Oooh, things can't be that bad. Here, I'll tell you a story about someone who really had it bad. A lad in a cell. Maybe sixteen years old. The judge asked him:

> "Tell me now, my little fellow,
>
> Have you bumped off many men?"
>
> "Just three of them were Christians
>
> Plus one hundred Yids and ten."
>
> "For the Yids we shall forgive you.
>
> For the Christians we shall not.
>
> Thus at dawn tomorrow morning,
>
> In the courtyard, you'll be shot."

"Isn't that pretty? What, you don't think so? Well, to be frank, neither do I. In America this could never happen. Everybody is always happy in America."

She started to cry and crumpled to the floor.

I tried the standard treatment of food and funny stuff, but I knew that nothing would work except a flower. I rummaged along the kitchen counter, under the table, and through the drawers in search of the bouquet, but it was nowhere to be found. I thought that maybe my mother had taken it with her to show to the neighbors at the barbershop. (She hadn't; years later, I would discover the withered stalks in the attic niche. They were arranged in an eerie semblance of two Hebrew letters, hai and yud, י ח , the symbol for life.)

Then I had a brainstorm. If I couldn't bring the flowers to the sister, I would bring the sister to the flowers. Better yet, I would put an end to her madness, not with one frail daisy, but a million. I would cure her with azaleas, pachysandras, lilies, peonies, snapdragons, and a thousand more varieties of bloom. I would take the nurseling to the nursery.

"How about a nice walk?"

She lay inert as I wrapped her in a quilt and propped her up in the curve of a wheelbarrow. I tied a bonnet under her pudgy chin like a noose of yarn around a wildflower's neck.

"See the trees," I said as I pushed her out the front door. "They're actually big flowers. The reason we have to pick little ones, you see, is that if we let all flowers grow into trees there wouldn't be enough room for people. Do you believe me?"

Polish soil was so fertile that it was the only European land to grow sugar beets in addition to the more easily cultivated oats, barley, and rye. Of course, these crops to feed a nation required vast fields, but a single, large building full of the same nutritious earth could raise enough flowers for our small population. This building was the greenhouse. It was an amazing edifice, a transparent glass triangle that remained upright without beams, maybe by magic. Old man Medisky, who guarded this secret, had retired into the study benches of the shul, while his son, Ed, was content to eke out a modest living. He and one non-Jewish laborer sowed and nurtured the shoots of carnations, gladioli, and amaryllis. His wife sold the mature blossoms from a stall in the market. People bought these flowers daily the way cosmopolites buy newspapers. Since every other person here was a gossip and the rest philosophers, we didn't need a paper. Information and opinion we had in abundance, but a tulip in mid-winter was a token of beauty for even the poorest and most wretched.

The greenhouse consisted of a series of glass panes that reminded me of a quilt. Instead of novel patterns, however, each square was identical to every other. The color of the glass this twilight was that of the gray sky but delineated from it by the lead strips that joined the panes and sealed the interior. The door, also glass, swung welcome. Although I had just purchased a bouquet that was born here, I had never been inside. I felt as if I were stepping into a diamond.

"Well," I said, "it's certainly warm."

That was putting it mildly. There were stoves every six feet in the aisle between halves of the jungle. Waves of heat spread upward as a mist filtered down from an elaborate sprinkler system. Terra-cotta pots and rectangular wooden boxes like open coffins were crammed into every available inch of table space. In each small plot a dozen plants vied for life. Leaves crawled over the planter walls and drooped into the aisles, and some vines crept up the lead binders of the windows, in which the reflected images of the tropical blossoms glowed.

My little sister's eyes were full of flowers. She lunged forward out of her seat into the aisle. Her pink swaddled form no higher than the tabletops was like a bunny in the fields. Tottering on, bumping left and right, she poked her nose into one plant after another, sniffing and giggling. She was flushed from the heat and the pleasure. Then her arm caught in a tangle of ivy, and she tore it free, but the tendrils clung like a green tattoo. Then she screamed.

One of the vines was alive.

My sister howled and spun like a dreidel. She had never seen a snake before, and she was terrified. Even I, who had calmly observed reptile life by the river, was shaken. Nevertheless, protector of the weak, I gripped the slimy, metallic tail and yanked it off. The viper slithered around the mound of earth my sister had upset, poked up its triangular head, hissed, and slid toward us.

"Back!" I stamped my foot; but the serpent advanced undaunted. It was, after all, at home. I was the intruder. The shock of the confrontation froze me. My sister's screams crazed me. I grew stubborn and determined to repulse the venomous brute.

I reached for the nearest weapon, the kerosene stove. My hands seared on contact. I pushed it with all my might.

And the stove crashed, and the kerosene poured from its iron grate, and the fire rolled across the floor. In seconds the entire bench was ablaze, the plants' leaves shriveling, blossoms curling, berries popping with brown spurts. The snake was a writhing cinder. The kerosene quickly burned off, but the wooden floor nourished the fire, which advanced on a second stove.

The danger obvious, I grabbed my sister and ran. We reached the door as the stove exploded and the rest followed suit in a hideous chain reaction. Instead of the steamy exhalations of the plants, smoke rose to the peak of the triangle, and a window burst with the heat. The booming sounds of the explosions were punctuated by the tinkling of breaking glass and the shouts of the people who came running to witness the conflagration.

Proszowicer converged on the burning greenhouse from all directions, especially that of the barbershop. I didn't quite realize the extent of the damage until then. I didn't know that the flames were towering like a church spire. I couldn't imagine that the whole town might be kindling. There was panic in the raging wind in the crimson light. One group formed a brigade to pass buckets of water along from the well in the square. Others hurled themselves at the foundation of the nursery with pickaxes or shovels. Fire was such a dread calamity that the community would pay to rebuild anything that burnt down, so the Mediskys were not ruined; but the old man sobbed at the stench of his flowery babies being consumed in their cradles. Still, he struck at the building he loved with the same implements he had used to construct it. Even his friends from the study benches rapped at the weakened glass with their canes.

The annihilation of the Proszowice nursery was a deep and hurtful offense to the spirit of every Jew. It was an insult from heaven that demanded an investigation. On the spot, a council was convened: my father and the Rabbi, a teacher, a tailor, and Ed Medisky, all smudged with ashes, the usual inquisitors. Blame was not their goal. Another, more potent motive impelled them—curiosity. The mere physical cause of the fire was insignificant, but it might help to understand why they had been called upon to make this sacrifice. With the still-glowing embers a constellation in the shattered remains of the diamond sky, the question was asked, "Why did this tragedy occur?"

I had been noticed leaving the scene of the fire shortly after it broke out. Had I seen anything suspicious?

"See anything?" I repeated dumbly, my blistered palms locked behind my back.

Yes, a stray cow, a lightning bolt, maybe somebody deliberately tilting a stove.

I was not a destructive type of boy. On the contrary, I had acted in bravery and benevolence, but there was no doubt that this terrible accident was my fault. My hands bore the mark of guilt. I could not lie, yet the inquiring eyes would not allow me to remain silent. I wanted to explain, but the words stuck in my throat. I coughed and cleared my throat, then I heard.

"Mmmm . . . eee."

Everyone turned.

My little sister was smiling, the pink tip of her tongue visible between the two incomplete rows of baby teeth. Her thumb was pointing proudly to her chest, a bright red flower sprouted beneath it. "Uhhh . . . I," she groaned. "Ffff . . . I . . . rr."

It was her first sentence. Even if the diction was faulty, the meaning was clear. It was impossible but undeniable. She repeated her gleeful confession, "Meee." She was Eve, giving recipes for apple cider. What was going on? Didn't I know? Couldn't I guess? Lying ran in the family.

QUESTION: I saw a man walking on his two legs, a lifeless man who never existed. How is this possible?

ANSWER: It was a reflection on water.

QUESTION: A stranger spoke to me without tongue or voice. He has never been and will never be. Who is he?

ANSWER: A dream.

The darker the night, the brighter the stars.
The deeper the pain, the closer to God.

Torguemada

am the Grand Inquisitor. My piercing Spanish eyes are wide with righteous indignation beneath my great black hood and cowl. I have the Jew in my grasp, but he refuses to recant. He assaults me with his spurious Hebrew logic. My mind storms at the sacrilege. I must restrain myself from wringing his neck like the chicken he resembles. Instead, I survey my armory of more persuasive implements and consider, with pleasure, which to use on this very special day: the tongs, the thumb screw, the rack, the fire. I sneeze.

This dungeon, my domain, is raw with winter. I can hear the wind rushing through the cracks between the enormous gray stones. Odors of mold and putrefaction are borne along like fish in the sea. Gusts find their way under my cassock, ripple my thighs like a horse's flanks. My arthritic fingers clutch Ecclesiastes to my chest, and I think that the Jew must suffer similar pangs without similar comfort. At least I am accustomed to this spiritual netherworld, while all he knows is his warm thatched cottage, homey with the moist heat and smell of his grandmother's soup. Not soon will he feast on beans and the blood of Christian children. Not soon will he escape the benevolent clutches of the Inquisition. I hold my lantern aloft to examine his fear, but when I sneeze again I drop it and the flame gutters and dies.

Despite the intense cold, I am sweating as I make my way down the darkened corridor. Is it the supernatural illumination that guides me through the pitch labyrinth beneath the castle which is burning me up from within or merely my hatred of the Jew? A fire out of control on a glacial slope, the extremes of temperature wrack and contort me to their whim. Tapping this bone this way and that bone that, they play upon my brittle spine like a musician. We undergo the same tortures, myself and the Jew, but it is a small price to pay for eternal salvation. Each howl of agony that drifts through the walls is bringing some lucky soul closer to God. I envy them. Then I feel it, an awesome winged presence in the corridor with me. A silent, dreadful, magnificent visitation. The Holy Ghost?

From somewhere in the midnight passage comes a voice. "Who are you?"

"Your faithful servant," I reply, and drop to genuflect.

"I see no servant of the God of the Cross," the angry voice intones. "I see only . . . a Jew."

A Jew? "No, no, my Lord. Here," I tear at my hood, but where the black crest was is a knitted skullcap. "Here," I rip my shirt to reveal the crucifix ever upon my heart, but in place of the penitential hairshirt is a flannel nightgown, and beneath it a star of David.

What a dream, what a terrible, frightening dream! I am back in my Toledo four-poster bed, Spanish lace hanging from its carved mahogany peaks. My red-cassocked junior brothers surround me, praying. Their voices are sweet, and far away, beneath my chamber, I can make out the restful undertone of the prisoners' cries. My court physician is in attendance, bending over me, peering intently through his gold-rimmed spectacles, attaching a leech to suck the fevered blood from my still pulsing forehead. I try to speak, but I have been too exhausted by my recent ordeal. Even now it is not over, and there is something wrong about these people I think I know so well. They are engaged in a hushed consultation, so I only hear fragments.

"A judgment."

"Raving since he got home."

". . . could have happened?"

Gradually their mellifluous Iberian accents become harsher, more guttural. Then their words themselves grow vague, then strange.

"On his way home from cheder."

"Church," I rasp to correct them.

"It was something the blacksmith's son said."

"The blackness. What the blackness said."

But they ignore me, so I scrutinize them. I catch a whiff of something fishy. My God, protect me, the court physician smells of herring! He is an imposter. I try to writhe from his insidious grip, but he and his aides hold me down. Sweat springs to my forehead, floods into my eyes, burns them with salt. I shut them against the pain and sight of the Jew.

It is not enough to banish the vision of treachery. Words come through, in Yiddish. Miraculously, I understand the infidel tongue. I reopen my eyes in wonder at their magic and in order to remember their faces on the day of retribution.

"Who was the last to see him?"

A man dressed as a schoolteacher answers, "The students all left together, but he ran ahead of the others. He often does."

"This wouldn't have happened if he were more friendly."

"So then Zevchik, the blacksmith's son, went up to him. There were words, then a fight."

"That Zevchik is a terror."

"Nonsense," a new voice declares. "When haven't young blacksmiths beat up young Jews? Zevchik is neither better nor worse than any Pole." This speaker's face is different from the others. It is less cared for but more caring. It is sensible, but it is also sensitive, and despite its lowly position on a straight-backed wooden chair in the corner it obviously commands a great deal of respect.

A mournful woman beside the chair sniffs, "He shouldn't fight." Her face is soft, madonnalike, haloed by a checkered handkerchief, but I will not allow myself to be seduced. It smells of soap and the other domestic chores of the faithless Jewish home.

The schoolteacher continues: "They were pulled apart, and he could hardly walk. Already he was crazy. So we brought him here, and he's been like this ever since."

The physician says: "I can find nothing drastically wrong with him. There are bruises but they're minor." He pulls the engorged slug off my forehead and drops it into a glass container, which he seals. "I don't usually advocate leeching, but in this case I thought there might be too much pressure on the brain. It will make him weak and light-headed, neither of which can hurt him more than his delirium."

Delirium, they say! Just because I can see through their pitiful masquerade they are desperate to convince me that I am mad. Endangered, yes, insane, never. I have fallen into the hands of Marranos, false converters, mockers of the sacrosanct baptismal ceremony. Pretending to be good Spaniards, they are merely cowards evading the snares of the Inquisition, secret Jews. I shall tear their disguises from them, strip them bare, flay them, burn them, and consecrate their ashes to the greater glory of Christ. "Jews!" I scream at them.

"Yes," the quiet man in the corner responds.

"Jews! Jews!" There is no worse insult.

"You are a Jew," he says.

"That's a filthy, degenerate lie. I was born to a sainted Christian woman, brought up in the household of the Lord, and have taken my place as the father of his earthly ministry...I am Torquemada."

Most everyone in the room blanches and starts back in horror. They cannot help but accord the truly righteous a certain esteem. I can see the effect my name has on all of them—except the one in the corner. He seems saddened but not fazed. He says, "Then Torquemada is a Jew."

I spring up and at his neck. My fingers are ten wriggling snakes reaching to sink their fangs through the soft flesh.

He does not move to defend himself. It is the other Jews who subdue me and tie me to the bed.

"A dybbuk," the mystic utters.

"No, a delirium," the rationalist maintains.

"Who," the woman hovering by the man in the corner pleads, "can help?"

First it is the doctor's turn. Besides leeching me he forces me to drink a vile liquid that tastes like tree bark. I feel it knotting my stomach, coursing through, and purging me from within. My pillow is drenched with sweat, but I will not succumb. When he lays hands on me, intruding on my privacy, I must endure the offense. Wrapped as securely as a baby in swaddling clothes, I have only my words. "Do you not see the error of your ways, Jew?

How dare you refuse to acknowledge the divinity of the one Lord above?"

As this is a matter for theology, the Rabbi steps in. He is an ugly, cantankerous old goat, a pious criminal. I can smell his beard and rank gabardine coat. I can smell the pungent reek of his faith, like rotting moss caught in a castle wind. "We are the ones who recognize the one Lord," he says. "It is you that divide him into three."

"The Trinity, most hallowed, most ineffable of mysteries. One in three, three in one. You cannot understand."

"Then how can we believe?"

"You claim to understand your Lord, Rabbi? A minor God he must certainly be."

The Rabbi steps warily about this bed that imprisons me, as if afraid that I might break loose. He explains, "No, we do not understand our Lord. His ways are beyond human comprehension. But we do know that he is One."

"As is mine," I tell him. "One in three, three in one. A mystery greater than yours. If there are two great mysteries, must not the greater be attributed to the greater God?"

The Rabbi tugs at his smelly beard, then replies, "Then why not one in five, five in one, one in a million, a million in one. the greater the mystery...."

I have underestimated him. He has a point. Stalemate. I try another tack. "And the words of Christ on the cross?"

"Moses in the wilderness."

"Saint Paul."

"Elijah."

"Pope Innocent III."

"The Baal Shem Tov."

"We can banter religious authorities all night, Rabbi, but how can you deny the lay opinion of the citizens of the world? How can you deny their choice, which has given the community of Christ to be fruitful and multiply while you shrivel in this Polish backwater? How can you deny history?"

"Truth is not a matter of majority rule. How could we other-wise deny the words of the ancients as to the circulation of the blood, the roundness of the earth. A minority with truth on its side will always prevail, must always deny."

I am exasperated. I cannot contain myself. "Your minority is a rag-ridden, flea-bitten race of whorish, usurious, inbreeding Christ-killers and should be exterminated."

The Rabbi sighs, "No doubt if you have anything to say about it, we shall."

"Yes, I can see such a day, and not so long from now. It will be a splendid day, bathed in light and blood. There, on the white shore of the eternal kingdom, the good people shall be gathered. At sea, aboard a raft as large as an ark, the total remains of international Jewry are tied one to the other. The angels demand an end to the pestilence. I am proud to dip my torch to the scattered bundles of straw, which crackle and smoke until the oils of the wood and the sinews of the flesh catch fire. The flames mount. The last blasphemous prayers to a pagan God are drowned by the hosannas of the righteous Christian multitude as the final glorious auto-da-fé sinks sizzling beneath the waves. Rid forever of the Jewish contagion, it shall be a day of universal thanksgiving and universal belief in the one true God."

They are mute, agape before the power of my vision. Again, it is only the quiet man in the corner who can summon the will to speak to me. He asks calmly, "Are you a priest or a prophet?"

I could confound the doctor, refute the Rabbi, but this strange man's soft-spoken questions are beyond my ability to scorn. I can see the marks of my hands on his neck. I feel obligated to explain as best I can, and I do so with surprising modesty, in a voice almost like his. "It comes upon me at times."

The man merely nods. He puts a hand on the shoulder of the sobbing woman with the sweet face. "Go. Lie down," he advises her, and where the ministrations of the Rabbi and the potions of the doctor had failed to soothe her, his words have an inspirational effect. She nods and leaves, and I almost feel sympathy until I choke it back and remember that these are the killers of my Lord. Nursing dreams of revenge, I fall asleep.

When I wake, the man is still beside me, watching me.

"How did you sneak up on me, Jew?" I demand, and the man's eyelids shut and his head bows beneath their weight into his hands, as if my words were a magical incantation turning his flesh to stone. "I asked you a question, Jew. Now answer me. I say, 'Answer!'"

He moves no more than he has over the long course of the night.

"Answer me, dammit! Do you know who I am?"

In a weak, weary voice he moans, "Torquemada."

"Who?"

The man's head perks up, like a dog on its master's return from school, his eyes suddenly bright. Tentatively, hopefully, he asks, "You're not Torquemada?"

"What is this gibberish you keep repeating? Of course I'm not," I say the alien name with distaste, "Torquemada!"

The man rises, arms outstretched as if to embrace me.

"I am Saladin, Caliph of Egypt, Armenia, Mesopotamia, and Palestine, Ruler of the East and Representative of Allah."

The man collapses in a heap at the foot of the decadent Western bedpiece I am confined to. I would prefer a straw pallet on a baked mud floor to this frivolous, womanly cushion, shackles to the leather thongs that coddle as they bind me, the dungeons of Christ to this Jewish notion of luxurious imprisonment.

The woman with the sad face comes rushing to the aid of the man on the floor. Kneeling beside him, she turns to me, and cries, "What have you done to him, you ungrateful child? What have you done to yourself?"

"I do nothing for myself. My life is in the service of Allah."

The Rabbi, newly entered with pie crumbs upon his beard, looks as if I have just condemned him to decapitation. "Why do you do this?" he whines.

The man on the floor whispers, "Leave him be." This is a curious type of charity he practices. Notwithstanding his moment of weakness, I have the feeling that he is the only one who is a worthy antagonist.

"What has happened to you?" I ask him. "We were born together in the desert of the patriarch Abraham. We are cousins, yet you have left our common inheritance. Your faces are white from lack of the nourishing sun. You have no strength, no stamina. You are no better than Christians."

He seems staggered by my accusation, but before he can respond I continue: "Look about you. A cottage instead of a tent, an oven instead of an open fire." At the mention of warmth the European cold comes through the walls to freeze me. "Look at this feather quilt," I chatter, "and the worst of it is that it may be necessary in this godforsaken climate. You may have managed to capture me, but you are the ones who are prisoners in your comfortable homes."

I strain against my bonds, but I no longer have the power to resist them. I am betrayed by my own muscles, which have sunk into and become as one with the jelly of the mattress. The color is draining from my face, and the extra flesh shrinking from the head of my penis. Circumcision is the last indignity; I am becoming Jewish, and I cannnot stand it. They are everything I despise. They are feeble and overintellectual, servile, cultish. They smell of the shop and the shul. Every one of them is as prematurely old as their race.

I think that we are born with our thoughts already dwelling in our brains. Try as we may to consider other points of view, we always return to the place where we started. I know in my blood that I must kill Jews, and that is all there is to that. We are family, but there are no more bitter hatreds than those among relations. Yes, there are reasons for this eternal enmity, their stubborn refusal to acknowledge the one true prophet, Mohammed, their pious stance that makes the rest of us feel like dirt, their ugly habits, their evil nature; but as sufficient as all this may be, it is also superfluous.

The main reason Jews must be killed is tautological, because they must be killed.

As if he can read my mind, the solitary man still on the floor asks a simple question, "And what will the world be like when you have killed all of us?"

The answer is so simple I cannot understand how he does not see it. "Why, it will be like a world without Jews."

The man nods sagely and returns to the chair to resume his vigil.

Night and day the man stays with me as I sleep to the fevered dreams of Judaism and wake to the might and glory of Jew-haters everywhere. I am Pharaoh, watching the pyramids rise on the mixture of limestone bricks and Hebrew sweat. I am Nebuchadnezzar sacking Jerusalem. I am Herod and I am Haman. I am Persian, Roman, Briton, and Turk. I am every prince or pope who has ever stoned or hung, drowned or burned the Chosen People. I am the proud persecutor ranging through the millennia, searching out my victims wherever they hide, for the taint of their blood always gives them away. The despised race always dies, but they always survive as a remnant that troubles my dreams.

The doctor and the rabbi must admit that I am too powerful for their meager talents to deal with, but given their one-track minds, they can only think to call in other doctors and rabbis. These celebrated men in three-piece suits and silver-rimmed pince-nez jab needles into me, infecting and extracting various vital fluids. They recommend diets and physical regimens. They mumble words of prayer and parade Torahs before me as though I were a sacrificial goat. They confront me with alleged teachers and neighbors and pallid bookworms whom they claim are the companions of the imaginary childhood they have constructed for me. One wants to beat me, saying, "A good switching is all he needs," while another dangles a gold watch idiotically back and forth in front of me. Whatever their remedy for whatever Semitic disorder they have attributed to me instead of themselves, they are equally flawed by their bad blood and incapable of effecting any change in me.

The only one I have a hard time with is the man in the corner, who, as far as I can tell, never leaves the room. It is small compensation that the rabbis also seem to have problems with this contemplative statue of a man. When urged to some violent action by one of his failed wonder-workers, he answers with a definitive incongruity that will brook no response, "The boy always had a good imagination."

Second only to the man is the woman who is frequently brought in and out of my cell, where she sobs, the self-made martyr of some private tragedy. Still, when one of her washerwoman companions makes a snide remark about me, the woman reins in her sorrow and answers, "At least he's eating."

Suddenly I have an idea. I understand why this couple does not disturb me as much as the others. They too are prisoners. She was my chambermaid, he perhaps an aged retainer. Now I have a plan. I bide my time, and when I am alone with them I whisper, "Listen, I know who you really are, and I know that you know who I really am, so help me escape. I will reward you with half of my kingdom."

But the man only mutters, "And I would reward you with my entire kingdom," and again we all lapse into a silence as deep as the ocean.

The woman's long-drawn-out sigh is like a bubble floating from the depths to break at the surface of that ocean. "I don't know," she says. "I just don't know where to turn." A hysterical note comes into her voice, and she yearns to leap. "We've had every Jew between here and Warsaw here, and none of them can help. What can we do?"

"Wait for the Lord, blessed be He," the man reasssures her, but despite himself he raises his eyes, entreating his Lord to stop taking his own sweet holy time and grant deliverance now. There is an ominous rumbling in the skies; the room grows dim. A ray of light pierces the dusk like a spear. It is as if the desired redemption has indeed come down from the heavens and struck the man between the eyes. He asks the woman to repeat herself.

She is baffled and hesitant. "I don't know where to turn?" she says phrase by halting phrase, like a youthful violinist. "I just don't know where to turn?"

"Yes. Yes. Go on."

"We've had every doctor and Rabbi and teacher and ev—"

"No," he cuts her off, "that isn't what you said." He has a strange wakeful gleam in his eye, like someone with a present hidden behind his back. "You said that we've had every Jew here."

She begins to look at him with the same concern that has so far been reserved for me. Warily, she asks, "So who else is there?"

"There are 'his' people."

"Goyim?" The word escapes with horror.

"One in particular . . . the Zevchik lad."

"The one who did this? No, no, I forbid it. You must be crazy too. No. Absolutely not."

"He can't have any worse reaction to Zevchik than he has to us. We have to."

A sallow, pimply youth is brought into my cell between the rabbi and the doctor. "You," I call to him. "Boots!"

He cringes, but he does not obey.

"Are you deaf, boy? I said that I wanted my boots, and I meant now. So shine them, wax them, buff them, and bring them before I have you spitted like a pig. . . . Don't just stare, and while you're about your task, bring my waistcoat, and also my saber, then saddle my horse. The time has come, don't you hear me, the time has come for action. Come on, snap to it! I don't have to tell you why this is necessary. They poison our wells. They steal children like yourself to make their filthy matzos. They have fortunes hidden to seduce our maidens, subvert our morals, and corrupt our race, these Rothschilds.

"But we won't let them. The international Jewish conspiracy must be smashed. It must be rooted out of the high places it has usurped and the low places in which it breeds. We shall start a pogrom that will inspire good men everywhere. God's cavalry shall charge out of the steppes into the shtetls, and raze them flat. Get my boots, boy, for today, in the name of our Holy Father the Tsar and dear Mother Russia, today, against the Jews, today shall ride Chmielnicki, the king of the Cossacks!"

The boy turns on his heel, but the man from the corner has risen in stealth and stands behind him like a wall. "Now tell me, son, exactly what happened between you."

"Don't say a word," I order.

"Don't be afraid," the man says, "and please don't be ashamed. We mean you no harm. You see we must find out what happened, and you're the only one who can tell us."

"Silence!" I am frightened as by none of the previous torturers. "Silence, I command you, silence, you peasant!"

"I cursed him," the boy mutters. "I called him a dirty Jew."

"Who are you calling a Jew?"

"Please go on."

"I said other things . . . I'm not sure. Whatever came to my mind. We always do. It's what we always do." His audience rapt, the boy becomes positively voluble. If I could I would strangle him, but I am trapped, and gnash my teeth fruitlessly. "Oh, he was a strange one," the boy says. "He actually asked me why I hated Jews. Then when I answered him we started fighting."

The calm voice makes one last query, "And what did you say?"

"I said it was a stupid question. I told him that he knew why we hate you . . . because you hate yourselves."

The boy chatters on, and the rabbis exchange views on this new profanity, but an overpowering silence emanates from the man. He ushers the boy to the door and nods goodbye to the rabbis. He seems to sleepwalk to my bed, and for the first time during my captivity I am afraid he may harm me. His expression wavers unnaturally, still it is his usual mournful tone that repeats to me, "because we hate ourselves."

I blurt out, "Because your God hates you."

"Why?"

"You need to ask why? Because of me, Chmielnicki, and because of Herod and Haman, and because of Torquemada. Or will you tell me that's how He shows His love?"

And I start to cry. I press my eyes shut, but the tears well up and squeeze through. I hold my breath, but sniffles choke me and I must gasp for air. I am a dam, leaking, cracking, crumbling, and with each tear I feel my ability to resist failing. My years seep away, and with each tear a Jewishness rises in me, and the more it grows the stronger it gets. Samson wasn't a Jew until Delilah cut his hair. The dam bursts, and the torrential flow of Jewish lamentation sweeps me out to sea, to drown if need be with the rest of my people. My power gone, I succumb to the pathetic traits of my race with a rush of pure joy. I am sobbing uncontrollably now, because I think that if He doesn't cry for us, someone has to, and it might as well be me.

"It's all right. It's all right now," the man with me repeats over and over again, working swiftly to untie the straps that hold me down, hugging me as I spring up. His arms around me are just as strong as but so much more secure than the straps, and his voice is understanding and wise and loving. "It's all OK. Maybe the Messiah's been a little late, maybe he'll be a little later, but Torquemada's gone, and we don't have to worry. We have each other and it's the twentieth century of civilized man. There, there. What harm could possibly come to us in 1928?"

Between sobs I manage to gulp, "Yes, Daddy."

AfterWord

When John Fowles's *The Magus* was due to be reprinted a dozen or so years after its initial publication, Fowles apparently said something like, "Wait. There are some things I'd like to change." This struck me as both astonishing and exemplary, because it meant that the book clearly was not dead to its author. Rather than sit back and count his royalties, he jumped at the chance to make a story he must have loved when he wrote it even better in the light of the skills he had developed over the intervening years.

Well, I'm not going quite that far—nor have the editors who are using the "camera ready copy" of the first edition of *Imaginary Childhood* offered me the chance—but the opportunity to reflect on my work of more than a decade ago is irresistible. Mind, I do not consider myself to be the best interpreter of my own writing. That's the province of critics and readers, so I'll just use this space to take pleasure in the notion that this book is about to have a new life and to recall what was going through my head as I wrote it.

In fact, I didn't know that I was writing *Stories of an Imaginary Childhood* for several years after I commenced it. All I knew was that during graduate school I had written one story set in the Polish shtetl of Proscowice, where my father had grown up before World War II. The story was "Sincerely, Yours" and how pleased I was by that oddly placed comma that defamiliarized the normal complimentary closure. Sideline here: when the book came out, my father claimed that this particular story was, at least in its loosest outlines, true, and that he was the protagonist. But whether I had heard the story over the dinner table ages before and subconsciously filed it away for future use or whether he read it and retroactively incorporated it into his memory doesn't make a difference. In some way, the story was alive for him, too, and that may be my greatest delight.

Anyway, it wasn't until a few years later that I returned to Proscowice while trying to write another story about a young would-be poet's encounter with an elderly poet. Eventually titled "New Words for Old," that story was set in the present on the stage of the 92nd Street Y in New York City, and no matter how I struggled, it refused to gel. Why I thought to relocate it in Proscowice I'm not sure, but the second I left the walnut-paneled auditorium on the Upper East Side and entered a decrepit Polish shul, the story immediately fit together.

Clearly this was fertile territory so I found myself writing story after story set in Proscowice until I began to actively seek out fictions that might belong. For example, "The Virtuoso" commenced with no plot, but rather with the sense that, given the emblematic significance of violins to European Jews, there ought to be a musical story available if my ears were sufficiently attuned to catch its melody.

Still, I didn't think of the growing pile of Proscowice stories as a whole even though they shared a unity of time and place and a single narrative perspective. They didn't cohere until the title now on the cover popped out of the blue—actually the red neon sign of the Sing Wu Chinese restaurant across Second Avenue from where I lived in a studio apartment atop a pawn shop, its three brass balls hanging outside my window (you know why the traditional sign of a pawn shop is three balls? because that's how many it'll take from a man—an afterword is an excuse for meandering). This process continued as I ordered the disparate stories and revised accordingly, inserting the main character of one into the background of another, aiming for an emotional continuity since I was not yet able to maintain the distinct narrative line of the novelist.

Perhaps the reason I couldn't find that single narrative is because it would have been intolerable. Or ineffable. Or unbearable. Or all of the above because it's the worst event in history, the Holocaust. At the same time as being drawn to the Holocaust for reasons of personal history and because writers always take interest in bad news, I am deeply suspicious of turning atrocity into art. Though I live in fiction, I'd prefer to leave the Holocaust to the realm of brute facts, figures, numbers, diagrams, train schedules. Therefore I didn't and still don't write about the years 1939 to 1945.

Unfortunately, time provides a poor boundary. Can one write about, say, New York in 1943? Of course. Well then, if the lines of respect for the dead are geographical, can one write about the shtetl but not the ghetto, the ghetto but not the camp, the camp but not the chamber? In *The Last of the Just*, Andre Schwarz-Bart goes into the chamber and does so out of aesthetic and moral necessity. Perhaps to be consistent, all I ought to say is not that *one* shouldn't write about the Holocaust, but that *I* can't write about it.

Yet of course I can't keep away, so I guess that I've granted myself a chronological dispensation. One of my later books, *After*, occurs immediately post-liberation and the book in front of you takes place prior to catastrophe. Yet even this distinction is logically dubious, because the War is obviously the enormous, unstated subject of *Imaginary Childhood*. Its shadow hangs over the book, and any sane reader ought to know what will happen to every single person in the book ten years after the last page.

Not that pre-War European Jewish life was a bowl of rubies. Only in comparison to the future was this kingdom of poverty, shabbiness, and ongoing oppression benign enough for an adolescent boy to bother worrying about girls and parents rather than whether he would live through the next day of German occupation.

More shocking is the notion that when I wrote *Imaginary Childhood* the world was more benign than at the moment in which I write these words. Right now Israel is beset by suicide murderers (a term I prefer to the more common and insidiously neutral "suicide bombers") and anti-Semitism is gloriously resurgent in Europe. I think back on the penultimate words of *Imaginary Childhood*, "What harm could possibly come to us in 1928?" Just change the digits and substitute 2002 . . . or 2003 . . . or 2004 . . .

We all eventually die, yet some of us have a chance to live a little first. That's the way it should be and virtually never is, at least not for Jews.

Will a Second Holocaust be some other writer's awful tale to tell? And will the telling make any difference? The answer to the first question is "We don't know," and the answer to the second is an explicit "No." But we do it anyway, because we don't know what else to do and because we cannot do otherwise.

New York City, May 2002